KB269939

15소년 표류기

Adrift in the Pacific

 DARAKWON

About Wise & Wide

- 렉사일 지수(Lexile® measures)에 맞춘 체계적인 6단계 영어 독서 프로그램
- 우리나라와 세계의 초등 교과 과정을 분석해 뽑은 다채롭고 흥미로운 주제
- 스토리, 설명문, 명작 리라이팅 등 다양한 형식의 새롭고 유익한 읽을거리
- 정보와 재미, 논픽션 학습과 픽션 학습의 장점을 한 번에!
- 탄탄한 독후 활동으로 쑥쑥 자라는 사고력

Wise & Wide는 렉사일 지수(Lexile® measures)를 기준으로 각 단계를 체계적으로 나눈, 총 60권 구성의 6단계 영어 독서 프로그램입니다. 렉사일 지수는 미국 정규 공교육 과정과 여러 영어 프로그램에서 가장 많이 사용되는 영어 독서 지수입니다. 미국 50개 주 가운데 21개 주에서 렉사일 지수를 학기말 시험(End of Grade) 성적표에 직접 표시하며, 세계적으로 저명한 300개 이상의 출판사들이 렉사일 지수를 채택하여 사용하고 있기도 합니다. 우리나라와 미국, 영국, 호주 등 세계 초등 교과 과정을 분석해 뽑은 흥미로운 주제로 미국, 영국의 우수한 작가들이 집필한 다양한 종류의 읽을거리를 만나보세요. 도표(organizer) 완성, 자기 생각 말하기, 독후 테스트 풀기 등 탄탄한 독후 활동도 준비되어 있습니다.

시리즈 수준 & 렉사일 지수

시리즈 단계	렉사일 지수	미국 학년 (U.S. Grade)
Level 1	200L 이하	Pre K - K
Level 2	190L - 400L	Lower Grade 1
Level 3	350L - 530L	Upper Grade 1
Level 4	420L - 650L	Grade 2
Level 5	520L - 940L	Grade 3 - 4
Level 6	830L - 1070L	Grade 5 - 6

* 똑똑한 영어 읽기 Wise & Wide 시리즈의 1단계는 미국의 미취학 수준에 해당합니다.
* 렉사일 지수와 미국 학년과의 관계 출처: CCSS(Common Core State Standards) FOR ENGLISH LANGUAGE ARTS, APPENDIX A (2012, 미국 45개 주에서 사용 중)

퍼즐처럼 다양한 Topic List

	Level 1	Level 2	Level 3	Level 4	Level 5	Level 6
1 권	과학>생물: 동물들의 겨울잠 Story	과학>생물: 생물과 무생물 Story	과학>생물> 동물, 환경: 해달 Story	환경> 자연과 인생: 해녀 & 감나무 Story	과학>생물> 동물: 아마존의 놀라운 동물들 Story	과학>생물: 세균, 전염성 질환 Story
2 권	문학>세계 명작: 이솝 우화 Story	문학>전래 동화: 돌에 관한 옛이야기 Story	사회>경제: 용돈 버는 사업, 저축 Story	과학>생물> 식물: 광합성 Story	과학>지구과학: 지각, 지진, 화산, 대기 Report	수학>수열: 황금 비율과 피보나치 수열 Story
3 권	과학>물리: 그림자의 원리 Story	문학>세계 명작: 피터 팬 Story	과학>과학 기술: 나노봇 Story	문학>신화: 세계의 천지 창조 이야기 Story	문학>전설: 아서왕 이야기 Story	문학>신화: 별자리 신화 Story
4 권	문학>전래 문학: 탈무드 Story	과학>생물> 동물: 북극곰 Story	과학>생물> 동물: 마운틴 고릴라 Story	사회>인류 문화: 세계의 놀라운 고대 문화 Story	과학>지구과학: 구름과 날씨 Story	문학> 인간과 동물: 소녀와 말의 우정 Story
5 권	사회>윤리: 생활 속의 규범 Story	과학>생물: 몸의 감각 Report	사회>인류 문화: 세계의 독특한 축제 Report	예술>음악: 오페라 이야기 Story	사회>세계 문화· 역사: 르네상스 시대의 특징 Story	스포츠> 보드 스포츠: 서핑 & 스노보딩 Story
6 권	사회>세계지리, 여행: 세계의 명소 Story	과학>생물> 동물: 공룡 Story	과학>천문학: 우주, 태양계 행성 Story	사회>인물: 고난을 이겨낸 세 위인들 Story	과학>과학 기술: 놀라운 로봇의 세계 Report	예술>음악: 낭만주의 시대의 작곡가들 Report
7 권	과학>우주 과학: 우주 비행사들의 생활 Report	사회>인류 문화: 세계의 전설 속 괴물들 Report	수학>기초 수학: 숫자, 측정, 형태, 데이터 Report	과학·사회> 기술, 문화: 세계의 발명품 Report	예술>미술: 세계의 명화 Report	사회>인간과 동물: 인간을 위해 활약하는 동물들 Report
8 권	사회>인류 문화: 세계의 다양한 생활 문화 Story	예술>음악: 오케스트라의 악기들 Story	사회>생활 안전: 조난 시 기본 대처 방법 Story	사회>역사: 미국의 골드러시 Report	사회·과학> 심리학: 생활 속의 심리학 Story	문학>세계 명작: 베니스의 상인 Story
9 권	사회>직업: 여러 직업에 관한 인터뷰 Report	과학>과학 기술: 시대의 변화와 기술의 발달 Story	사회>정치>선거: 학생회장 선거 Story	문학>세계 명작: 셜록 홈즈 이야기 Story	문학>세계 명작: 15소년 표류기 Story	
10 권		스포츠> 겨울 스포츠: 동계 올림픽 종목의 이모저모 Report		스포츠>구기 종목: 인기 있는 구기 종목의 이모저모 Report		

* 똑똑한 영어 읽기 Wise & Wide 시리즈는 60권까지 계속 출간됩니다.

How to Use This Book

●Before Reading

어떤 분야, 어떤 종류의 이야기를 읽게
될지, 줄거리는 어떠한지 미리 쉽게 알아
볼 수 있어요.

●영어 본문

미국, 영국의 우수한 작가들이 집필하여
각 단계의 수준에 맞는 영어 문장·표현
의 참맛을 제대로 느낄 수 있어요.

●Pop Quiz

쪽지 시험처럼 핵심을 찌르는 퀴즈로
해당 페이지의 내용을 잘 이해하고 있는
지 바로 확인해 보세요.

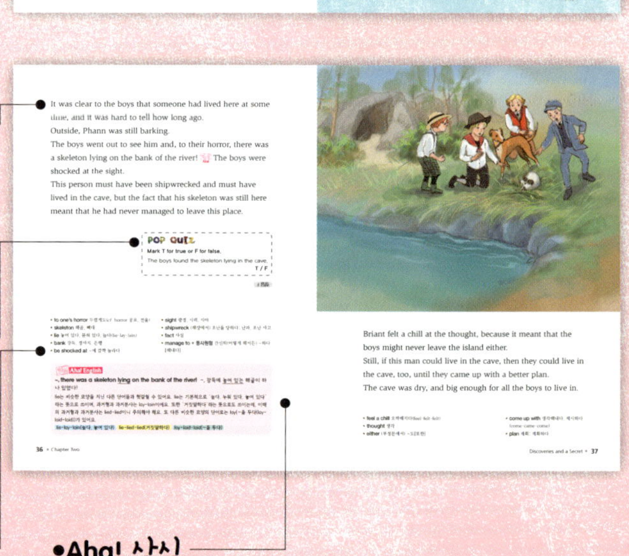

●어휘 설명

일일이 사전을 찾아보지 않아도 주요
어휘와 표현의 뜻을 알 수 있어요.

●Aha! 상식

Aha! 표시가 붙어 있는 문장에 대한 설명은 여기서 확인하세요.
문화 상식, 영어 구문이나 문법 상식, 그리고 과학·경제 상식까지!
각 분야의 상식들이 알차게 들어 있어 읽는 재미가 두 배예요.

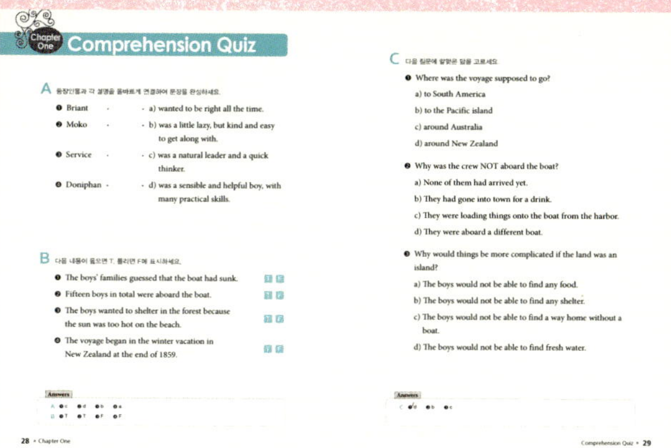

•Comprehension Quiz

한 chapter를 다 읽은 후에는 다양한 문제를 풀어보며 내용을 제대로 이해했는지 정리하고 넘어가세요.

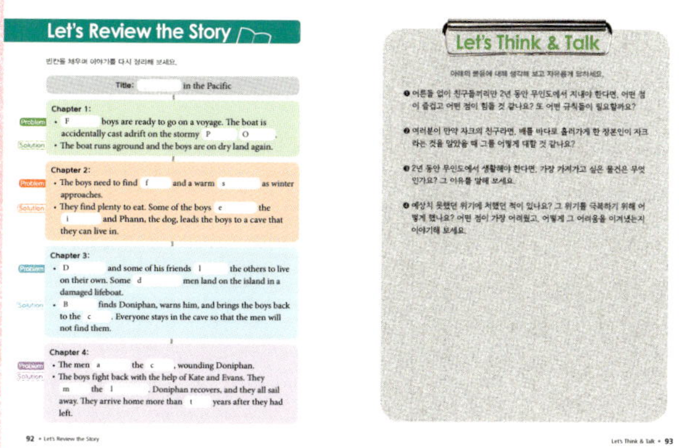

•Let's Review the Story /
•Let's Think & Talk

Organizer의 빈칸을 채우며 전체 이야기를 요약하고, 질문에 답하며 내 생각과 느낌을 자유롭게 정리해 봐요. 훗날 논술에 대비할 논리력과 사고력을 기를 수 있어요.

Audio CD

책의 내용이 그대로 담긴 오디오 CD. 오디오 극장처럼 생생하고 재미있는 음원을 만나보세요. (MP3 파일 PC·모바일 무료 다운로드)

온·오프라인 독후 테스트 & 온라인 단어 퀴즈·단어 리스트

독후 테스트는 책 또는 온라인으로 풀어볼 수 있어요. 온라인으로 풀면 좀 더 자세한 응시 결과와 함께, 전체 응시자들과 비교했을 때 내 실력이 어느 정도 위치인지도 알아볼 수 있어요.
추가로 제공되는 온라인 단어 퀴즈도 풀어보시고, 단어 리스트도 PC나 모바일로 무료로 다운로드 받으세요.

www.darakwon.co.kr

Before Reading

Adrift in the Pacific
15소년 표류기

Level 5-9,
Lexile®830L

•문학〉세계 명작
•story

기발한 상상력의 거장, 쥘 베른의 〈15소년 표류기〉

여러분은 만약 조난을 당해 무인도에 가게 된다면 과연 그곳에서 얼마나 버틸 수 있을까요?

여기 무인도에서 열다섯 명의 아이들끼리 무려 2년 동안 생존했다는 흥미로운 이야기가 있어요. 바로 19세기의 프랑스 작가 쥘 베른(Jules Verne)의 작품 〈15소년 표류기〉예요. 쥘 베른은 〈15소년 표류기〉 외에도 문학적 이야기에 과학적 공상을 더한 〈해저 2만 리〉, 〈80일간의 세계 일주〉 등의 작품으로 지금까지도 널리 사랑받고 있어요. 그는 다양한 작품에서 원자력 잠수함, 해저 여행, 달나라 여행 등을 다뤘는데, 놀랍게도 실제로 다음 세기에 이것들이 실현되면서 과학의 미래를 잘 예측했다는 평가를 받기도 한답니다. 〈15소년 표류기〉의 소년들은 혼자였다면 절대 할 수 없었을 어려운 일들을 친구들과의 협동을 통해 해결해 나가요. 이 책을 통해 그들의 도전 정신과 모험심, 갈등 상황에서도 서로 양보하는 배려심을 배워보세요.

❖ 원작의 프랑스어 제목을 영어로 번역하면 Two Years' Vacation이나, 본 책은 1889년 영국에서 출간된 영어본 축약판 Adrift in the Pacific을 토대로 각색하였기에 원제도 이렇게 표기해 둡니다.

줄거리

뉴질랜드 체어맨 기숙학교에서 14명의 소년은 여름방학 동안 뉴질랜드 전역을 항해하는 여행에 선발돼요. 출항하기 하루 전 모두가 배 안의 선실에서 잠든 그때, 항구에 정박해 있던 아이들이 탄 배가 무슨 이유에서인지 바다로 떠밀려 가게 되죠. 14명의 학생과 수습 선원 모코까지 총 15명의 소년은 며칠 동안 폭풍우 치는 바다 한가운데서 서로 힘을 합쳐 버텨내며 마침내 어느 무인도에 도착해요. 섬에 도착한 후 이들은 머무를 곳을 찾고, 지도자를 뽑아 하나의 작은 사회를 이루며 생활하게 돼요. 이 과정에서 서로를 미워하게 되거나 갈등이 생기기도 하지만 협동심을 발휘해 지혜롭게 헤쳐 나가요. 그런데 또 다른 난파선의 선원들이 이들을 발견하고는 공격하려 해요.

과연, 15명의 소년은 새로운 적을 물리치고 섬을 무사히 빠져나갈 수 있을까요?

Contents

Adrift in the Pacific

15소년 표류기

15소년 표류기

Adrift in the Pacific

Chapter One

A Storm and a Strange Land

폭풍우와 낯선 땅

It was the summer vacation in New Zealand at the end of 1859, and fourteen boys were all very excited.

They all attended a school in New Zealand for the sons of wealthy families, and had been chosen to go on a sea voyage.

They were going to cruise around the whole of New Zealand to advance their education.

The voyage was expected to take six weeks. The boys couldn't think of a better way to spend their vacation!

On the boat, there was a crew of seven sailors. There was also a cook, and a boy called Moko. He was a servant on the boat.

When the boys went aboard the boat, most of the crew had gone into town for a drink. The captain wasn't there yet. Only Moko and one sailor were there to greet them.

Once the boys were in bed, the sailor left Moko in charge and he went into town, too. But Moko was too tired to stay awake.

- **strange** 낯선, 이상한
- **land** 땅, 육지; 착륙하다
- **New Zealand** 뉴질랜드
- **at the end of** ~의 말에[마지막에]
- **attend** (~에) 다니다, 참석하다
- **wealthy** 부유한
- **choose** 선택하다(choose-chose-chosen)
- **go on a sea voyage** 바다 여행을 떠나다
  (cf. voyage 여행, 항해)
- **be going to + 동사원형** ~할 예정이다[것이다]
- **cruise** 유람선을 타고 다니다, 순항하다; 유람선 여행
- **whole** 전체; 전체의
- **advance** 증진시키다, 전진하다; 발전
- **education** 교육
- **be expected to + 동사원형** ~할 것으로 예상되다
  (cf. expect 예상하다, 기대하다)
- **take** (시간이) 걸리다, 데리고 가다(take-took-taken)

- **week** (일주일의) 주
- **better** 더 나은(good의 비교급)
- **crew** (배나 항공기에서 일반) 승무원(전원), 동료
- **sailor** 선원
- **servant** 하인, 부하
- **go aboard** (배·기차·비행기 등에) 탑승하다
  (cf. aboard 승선하여)
- **go for a drink** 술을 마시러 가다(go-went-gone)
- **captain** 선장
- **yet** (부정문·의문문에서) 아직, 거기에 또
- **greet** 환영하다, 인사하다
- **once** ~하자마자, 한때
- **leave** 남겨두다, 떠나다(leave-left-left)
- **in charge** ~을 맡은
- **too ~ to ...** 너무 ~해서 …할 수 없다
- **stay awake** 자지 않고 깨어 있다(cf. stay 머무르다)

Somehow, the rope that tied the boat to the harbor wall became unfastened. Nobody noticed the boat slipping out onto the water.

Moko was the first to wake up, and he shouted as loud as he could to wake up the others. Gordon, Briant, Doniphan, and a few others woke up. They called for help, but they were too far away for anyone to hear them.

The wind pushed the boat right out to sea, toward the Pacific Ocean. The boys saw a light coming toward them and yelled for help. It was a steam ship, huge and noisy.

Nobody aboard noticed the tiny boat or heard the boys' cries above the noise of their own engine.

- **somehow** 왜 그런지 모르겠지만, 웬일인지, 어쨌든
- **tie** 묶다, 속박하다(↔ untie 풀다)
- **harbor** 항구, 피난처
- **become** ~이 되다(become-became-become)
- **unfastened** 풀린, 묶지 않은
- **nobody** 아무도 ~않는
- **notice** 알아차리다, 주목하다; 공지
- **slip out** 미끄러지듯 나가다
- **shout** 소리 지르다
- **as loud as** ~만큼 시끄러운
- **call for** 요청하다(cf. call 부르다, 큰소리로 말하다)

- **far away** 멀리 떨어져
- **the Pacific Ocean** 태평양
- **light** 빛; (날이) 밝은, 가벼운
- **yell** 고함치다, 외치다
- **steam ship** 증기선(증기 기관으로 움직이는 배)
- **huge** 거대한
- **noisy** 시끄러운
- **tiny** 매우 작은
- **above** (소리가) ~보다 더 잘 들리는, ~위에(↔ below 위치가 ~보다 아래에)
- **engine** 엔진, 증기 기관

The steam ship came so close to the boys' boat that it knocked off a piece of the nameboard. 
Luckily, the small boat stayed upright instead of sinking, but the steam ship sailed past… and the boys sailed on into a rising storm.

Of course, the boys' families searched for them, but when they found the piece of nameboard, they guessed that the boat had sunk. Broken-hearted, they gave up the search.

정답 F

- **so ... that ~** 너무 …해서 ~하다
- **knock off** (~을 두드려) 떨어뜨리다, 중단하다
- **piece** 조각
- **nameboard** (배 등의) 이름을 적은 표지판, 간판
- **luckily** 다행히도, 운 좋게
- **upright** 똑바른, 꼿꼿한
- **instead of** ~ 대신에
- **sink** 가라앉다, 침몰시키다(sink-sank-sunk)
- **sail** 항해하다; 돛
- **rising** 거세지는(cf. rise 거세지다; 상승)
- **search for** ~을 찾다(cf. search 찾다; 찾기, 수색)
- **guess** 추측하다; 추측
- **broken-hearted** 가슴이 미어질 듯한, 슬픔에 잠긴
- **give up** 그만두다, 단념하다(give-gave-given)

- **several** 몇몇의
- **find oneself** ~한 상황에 처하다, (깨닫고 보니) ~에 있다(find-found-found)
- **yet another** (지금까지 나온 것들에 이어) 또 다른
- **endurance** 인내, 지구력
- **through** ~을 관통하여
- **crashing** 두려울 만한, 완전한, 최고의
- **rough** 거친, 개략적인, 난폭한
- **nothing to do but + 동사원형** ~할 수밖에 없다
- **hold on (to)** (~을) 계속 붙잡고 있다, (위험·곤란한 상황에서) 참아내다(hold-held-held)
- **tight** 단단히, 팽팽하게; 단단한, 촘촘한, 꽉 찬
- **tear** 찢어지다, 찢다(tear-tore-torn)

Several weeks later, the boys found themselves in yet another storm.

Each day was a test of endurance as the boat sailed on through the crashing waves.

When the weather was rough like this, there was nothing to do but hold on tight and hope that the sails would not tear.

스쿠너(schooner)와 증기선(steam ship)

두 개 이상의 돛대에 세로돛을 달고 바람의 힘으로 움직이는 서양식 배를 스쿠너(schooner)라고 해요. 이야기 속 아이들이 타고 있는 배가 이 스쿠너 형태예요. 15소년들 쪽으로 멀리서 다가오던 거대한 배는 증기선으로 증기 기관(수증기의 열에너지를 기계적인 일로 바꾸는 장치)의 힘으로 움직이는 배예요. 바람이 불지 않으면 움직일 수 없는 스쿠너 형태의 배와 달리 증기선은 운항이 확실히 보장되었어요. 세계 최초로 증기선을 이용하여 정기 항로를 개설하고 상업적으로 성공해 증기선의 시대를 연 사람은 미국 펜실베이니아의 풀턴(Robert Fulton)이에요.

On the deck stood Gordon, Briant, Doniphan, and Moko, all trying to steer the ship by holding onto the wheel. Doniphan looked white with fear, while Moko's skin was as dark as the clouds above them. These four were all aged between twelve and fourteen.

In the rooms below the deck were eleven younger boys and a dog.

- **deck** (배의) 갑판
- **stand** 서다, 견디다(특히 부정문·의문문에서 싫어함을 강조), 참다 (stand-stood-stood)
- **try to + 동사원형** ~하려고 애쓰다
- **steer** 조종하다, 이끌다, 나아가다
- **wheel** 타륜(배의 키를 움직이는 손잡이 달린 바퀴 모양의 장치), (자동차의) 핸들

- **fear** 두려움, 공포
- **while** 한편, ~하는 동안
- **aged** 나이가 ~(살)의
- **between** ~ 사이에, 가운데
- **suddenly** 갑자기
- **peer** 주의해서 보다, 응시하다
- **gloom** 어둠, 우울
- **question** 의심하다, 질문하다; 질문

- **lord** (영국에서 귀족을 칭하는) 경
- **certainly** 틀림없이 (*cf.* certain 확실한)
- **seem** (~인 것처럼) 보이다
- **reply** 대답하다
- **mast** (배의) 돛대
- **strip** 좁고 기다란 육지·바다 등
- **horizon** 수평선, 지평선

Suddenly, Moko yelled, "Land! I can see land!"

"Are you sure?" asked Doniphan, peering through the early morning gloom.

He always questioned everything that other people said, wanting to be right. Some of the others called him 'Lord Doniphan' because he certainly seemed to think that he was better than everyone else.

"Yes, I'm certain," replied Moko. "Look, to the right of the mast."

"It is land!" cried Briant. "It really is!"

Then, they all saw a long, low strip of land on the horizon.

Briant was a natural leader and a quick thinker. He reasoned
that if the boat was going to crash onto any rocks, everyone
would be safer on deck.

He opened the door that led down to the rooms below the
deck, and yelled, "Come up on deck, all of you."
Immediately, the dog jumped out and all eleven boys
followed.

The youngest ones began to scream when they saw the
waves around them.

Suddenly, there was a great thud. The boat had run aground on the rocks. Waves swirled around it and lifted it clear again, but they only carried it further in and dumped it onto some sand in shallow water.

The boat had reached the land, but what kind of land was it? It could be a continent, in which case they could travel overland until they reached some kind of settlement such as a village or town.

But if it was an island, things would be more complicated because there was no way of leaving without a seaworthy boat.

- **natural** 타고난, 자연의, 자연스러운
- **leader** 리더, 지도자
- **quick thinker** 머리 회전이 빠른 사람
  (*cf*. quick 빠른)
- **reason** 판단하다, 추론하다; 이유
- **crash (onto)** 충돌하다, 꽝음을[요란한 소리를] 내다
- **safer** 더 안전한(safe의 비교급)
- **lead down to** ~로 이어지다(lead-led-led)
- **immediately** 곧바로
- **follow** 따라오다, 뒤따르다
- **youngest** 가장 어린(young의 최상급)
- **begin** 시작하다(begin-began-begun)
- **scream** 비명을 지르다; 비명
- **thud** (둔탁한 소리) 쿵, 탁
- **run aground** (배가) 좌초하다(run-ran-run)
- **swirl** 소용돌이 치다, 빙빙 돌다; 소용돌이
- **lift** 들어 올리다
- **clear** 완전히, (~에서) 떨어져[닿지 않게]; 확실한

- **carry** 나르다
- **further** (거리상으로) 더 멀리, 한층 더
- **dump** (아무렇게나) 내려놓다, 버리다
- **shallow** 얕은
- **reach** 닿다, 도착하다
- **continent** 대륙
- **travel** 이동하다, 여행하다
- **overland** 육로로; 육로의
- **until** ~까지
- **settlement** 촌락, 거주
- **such as** ~와 같은
- **village** 마을
- **island** 섬
- **things** 상황, 형편
  (*cf*. thing (개인 소유나 특정 용도의) 물건)
- **complicated** 복잡한
- **without** ~ 없이
- **seaworthy** 항해하기 적합한

The boys scrambled out of the boat and waded ashore,
pulling the boat with them so that it was out of the water.
It was battered and broken up, so there was no way of sailing
away from here. The shore was deserted.

- **scramble** 재빨리 움직이다
- **wade** (물·진흙 속을) 헤치며 걷다
- **ashore** 해안으로[에], 물가로
- **so that** ~하도록

- **battered** 박살 난, 닳은
- **break up** 부서지다(break-broke-broken)
- **shore** (바다·호수 따위) 기슭, 해안
- **deserted** 사람이 살지 않는, 버려진, 황폐한

"First, we need food and shelter," said Briant. "Then, we can work out what to do next."

Briant and Gordon walked up the beach and into the forest, where they found a cliff. They followed the cliff until they reached a stream.

On the other side of the stream was a marsh. It was clear that there was no place to shelter there.

Disappointed, the boys returned to the wrecked boat. They would have to shelter there for now.

Fortunately, the bedding, clothes, and cooking things were still on the boat. There was even food, which Moko made into a good meal.

- **shelter** 피난처, 거처; (비바람·위험 등을) 피하다
- **work out** 해결하다, 운동하다
- **cliff** 절벽
- **stream** 개울
- **on the other side of** ~의 반대편에
- **marsh** 습지, 늪
- **disappointed** 실망한, 낙담한
- **return** 돌아오다, 돌아가다

- **wrecked** 난파된, 망가진
- **have to + 동사원형** ~해야 하다
- **for now** 당분간, 우선은
- **fortunately** 다행히
- **bedding** 침구(류), 잠자리
- **still** 여전히, 그럼에도 불구하고; 고요한
- **meal** 식사

Aha! English

It was clear that there was no place to shelter there. 거기에는 비바람을 피할 장소가 없는 것이 확실했다.

to부정사(to + 동사원형)는 문장 안에서 명사, 형용사, 부사 등 다양한 역할을 해요. 위 문장에서는 형용사적 용법으로 명사 뒤에 위치해 앞의 명사를 꾸며주고 있어요. '장소(place)'인데 '비바람을 피할(to shelter)' 장소라는 뜻으로 쓰인 거예요.

ex. I don't have any reason to tell him. 내가 그에게 말할 이유는 없다.

Moko was a very sensible and helpful boy, with many
practical skills that he used to make everyone safe and
comfortable.

Everyone seemed to be surprisingly cheerful, except Briant's
younger brother, Jack, who was quite miserable.

Next morning, the boys looked at their food supplies.

Briant and Gordon judged that they had enough to last for
two months, but they didn't know how long they might have
to survive in this place, so they needed to find other sources
of food.

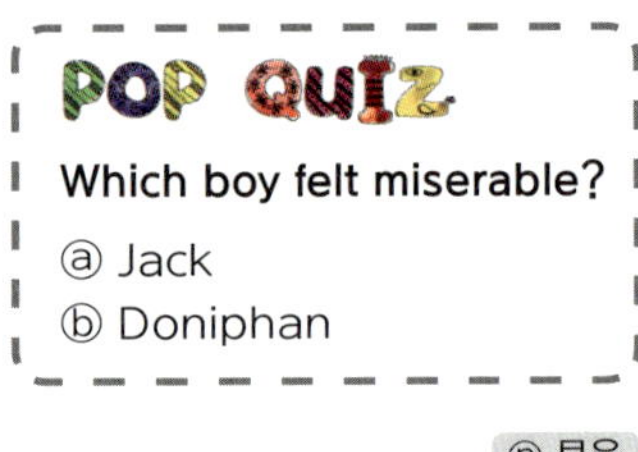

- **sensible** 분별 있는, 합리적인
- **helpful** 도움이 되는
- **practical** 실용적인, 현실적인, 유용한
- **skill** 능력, 기술
- **used to + 동사원형** ~하곤 했다,
  과거에는 ~이었다[했다]
- **comfortable** 편안한
- **surprisingly** 놀랄 만큼, 의외로
- **cheerful** 명랑한
- **except** ~을 제외하고는

- **quite** 꽤, 상당히
- **miserable** 슬픈, 비참한
- **food supply** 식량 공급(*cf.* supply 비축(량),
  보급 (물자); 공급하다)
- **judge** 판단하다; 판사
- **enough** 필요한 만큼, 충분히; 충분한
- **last** 견디다, 지속되다; 지난
- **might + 동사원형** ~일지도 모른다
- **survive** 생존하다, 견뎌내다
- **source** 원천, 근원

They gathered the eggs of seabirds and caught some fish using the fishing lines from the boat. They also found shellfish on the rocks near the sea.

As well as food, there were other supplies on board, such as ropes, sails, maps, and matches. There were plenty of warm, waterproof clothes.

There were also some guns, though Briant hoped that they would never have to use those!

They decided that they must try to find shelter in the forest. The weather on the beach was too wild, and they could not stay there when winter came.

- **gather** 모으다, 모이다
- **seabird** 바닷새
- **catch** 잡다(catch-caught-caught)
- **fishing line** 낚싯줄
- **shellfish** 조개류, 갑각류
- **as well as** ~뿐만 아니라, 게다가
- **board** 선내, 갑판, 이사회; 승선하다

- **match** 성냥, 시합
- **plenty of** 많은
- **waterproof** 방수의
- **though** 비록 ~일지라도
- **decide** 결정하다, 결심하다
- **wild** 거친, 야생의

Briant, Doniphan, Service, and Wilcox set out to explore, taking the dog, Phann, with them.

Gordon, who was very sensible, stayed behind to look after the other boys.

Service was a good-hearted boy, a little lazy but generally kind and easy to get along with.

The four explorers set off along the beach. They climbed up the cliff with some difficulty, and scrambled down the other side, where they found more forest. The boys walked and walked. The forest seemed to have no end.

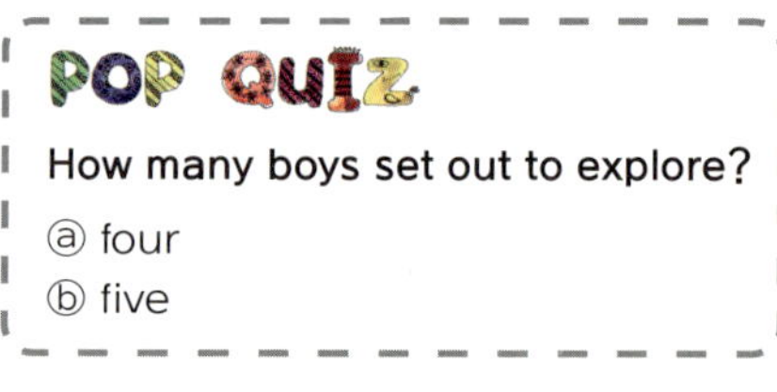

ⓔ 吕&

- **set out** 출발하다, (여행을) 시작하다(set-set-set)
- **explore** 답사하다, 탐사하다
- **stay behind** 뒤에 남다, 출발하지 않다
- **look after** ~을 돌보다
- **good-hearted** 친절한, 착한
- **generally** 일반적으로, 대개
- **get along with** ~와 잘 지내다[어울리다] (get-got-gotten)(cf. along ~ 을 따라서)
- **set off** 출발하다, (폭탄 등을) 터뜨리다, (비상벨 등을) 울리다

- **difficulty** 어려움, 고난
- **in the middle of** ~의 가운데에
- **come across** ~을 우연히 마주치다, 이해되다
- **make a discovery** 발견하다 (cf. discovery 발견)
- **a sort of** ~의 종류
- **wash** ~에 밀려오다, 휩쓸어 가다
- **suggest** (간접적으로) 말하다, 제안하다
- **prove** 증명하다
- **nearby** 바로 가까이에

In the middle of the forest, they came across a river, where they made a surprising discovery.

"Look at this," said Service as he peered at some rocks. "Someone has made a sort of bridge with these rocks."

"The rocks could have been washed there by a storm," suggested Briant. "It doesn't prove that there are people nearby."

But the boys were very watchful that night as they settled down to camp in the forest. They decided not to make a fire, in case there were people around. They didn't want to attract anyone's attention, but it meant that they spent a very cold night outside, with only cold food to eat.

The next morning, the boys woke up early and went a little way into the forest to explore it. To everyone's surprise, they discovered that they had been sleeping close to a hut made out of leaves and wood.

- **watchful** 주의 깊은, 경계하는
- **settle down** (조용히 한 곳에 사리잡고) 정착하다, 편안히 앉다[눕다](*cf.* settle (내려) 앉다, 머물다)
- **camp** 야영하다; 야영, 캠핑
- **make a fire** (모닥불을) 피우다
- **in case** 만약 ~인 경우에는, ~한 경우에 대비하여
- **attract** (주의를) 끌다, 끌어당기다
- **attention** 주의, 집중
- **mean** 의미하다(mean-meant-meant)
- **to one's surprise** 놀랍게도

- **discover** 빌견하다
- **close to** 아주 가까이에서
- **hut** 오두막
- **made out of** ~로 만든
- **leaves** 나뭇잎(leaf의 복수형)
- **surely** 확실히, 분명히
- **whisper** 속삭이다, 귓속말을 하다
- **as though** 마치 ~인 것처럼
- **anxiously** 근심[걱정]하여
- **cannibal** 식인종

Aha! English

~, "and we don't know if they are good or bad." ~, "그리고 우리는 그들이 착한지 나쁜지도 모르잖아."

if는 '만약 ~라면'이라는 뜻으로 가정을 할 때 쓰기도 하지만 위의 문장처럼 '~인지 아닌지'의 뜻으로 쓰기도 해요. 이때 if는 whether와 바꿔 쓸 수도 있어요.

ex. I wonder if he will come back tomorrow. 나는 그가 내일 돌아올지 안 올지 궁금하다.

"Surely that means that there are people nearby." whispered
Doniphan.

"The hut looks old, as though it has not been used for a long
time," said Briant.

"But there might be people around," said Service, anxiously,
"and we don't know if they are good or bad."

"I hope they aren't cannibals." whispered Wilcox.

Comprehension Quiz

A  등장인물과 각 설명을 올바르게 연결하여 문장을 완성하세요.

❶ Briant • • a) wanted to be right all the time.

❷ Moko • • b) was a little lazy, but kind and easy to get along with.

❸ Service • • c) was a natural leader and a quick thinker.

❹ Doniphan • • d) was a sensible and helpful boy, with many practical skills.

B  다음 내용이 옳으면 T, 틀리면 F에 표시하세요.

❶ The boys' families guessed that the boat had sunk. T F

❷ Fifteen boys in total were aboard the boat. T F

❸ The boys wanted to shelter in the forest because the sun was too hot on the beach. T F

❹ The voyage began in the winter vacation in New Zealand at the end of 1859. T F

Answers

A ❶ c ❷ d ❸ b ❹ a
B ❶ T ❷ T ❸ F ❹ F

 다음 질문에 알맞은 답을 고르세요.

❶ Where was the voyage supposed to go?

   a) to South America

   b) to the Pacific island

   c) around Australia

   d) around New Zealand

❷ Why was the crew NOT aboard the boat?

   a) None of them had arrived yet.

   b) They had gone into town for a drink.

   c) They were loading things onto the boat from the harbor.

   d) They were aboard a different boat.

❸ Why would things be more complicated if the land was an island?

   a) The boys would not be able to find any food.

   b) The boys would not be able to find any shelter.

   c) The boys would not be able to find a way home without a boat.

   d) The boys would not be able to find fresh water.

Answers

C ❶ d ❷ b ❸ c

Chapter Two

Discoveries and a Secret

발견한 것들과 비밀

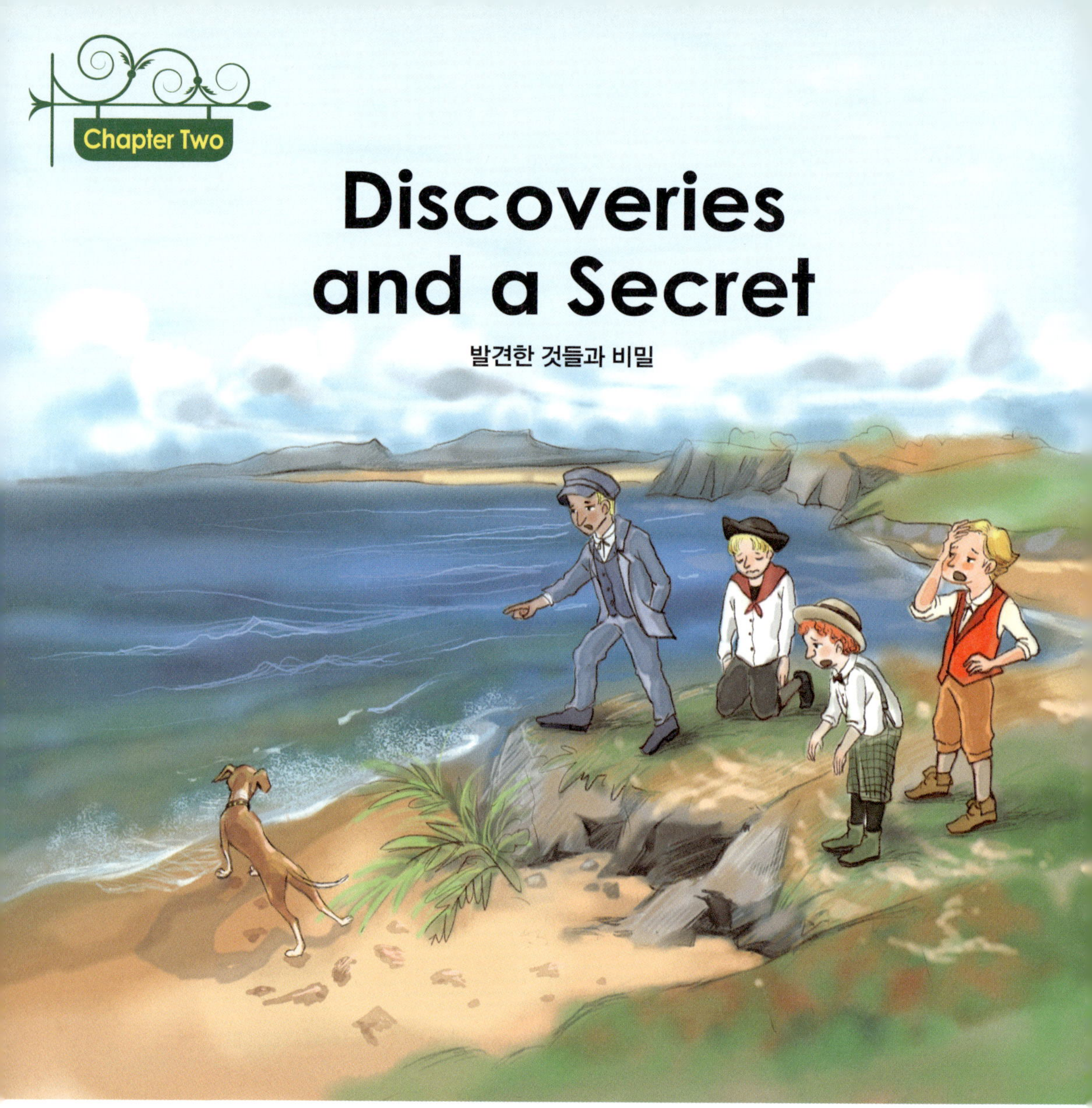

The boys finally came to the end of the forest, and beyond it they found a sandy beach and a huge expanse of water.

"It is an island," exclaimed Briant, half sick with disappointment.

"Look, here is the sea and there is no sign of a shore on the other side."

"I don't agree," said Doniphan, who didn't agree with Briant on much at all. "I think we should explore a bit further."

Even though Briant was getting increasingly angry with Doniphan and his argumentative ways, he agreed.

The boys set off again, looking warily around them for wild animals or people.

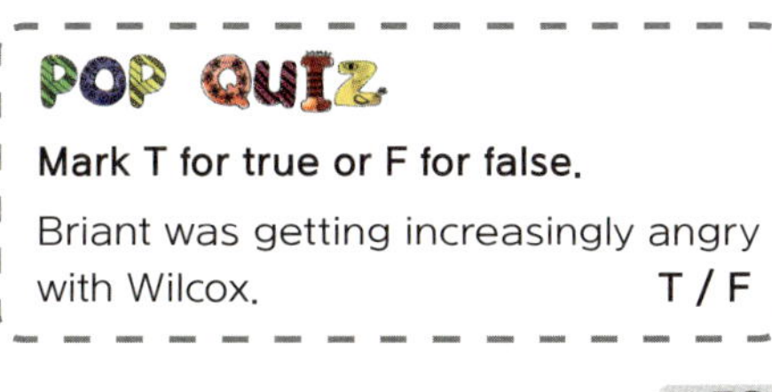

정답: F

- **secret** 비밀
- **finally** 마침내, 마지막으로
- **beyond** ~ 너머, ~ 이상
- **sandy** 모래로 뒤덮인
- **expanse** 넓게 트인 지역
- **exclaim** 소리치다, 외치다
- **half** 꽤, 다소, 반쯤
- **sick** 실망하여, 울화가 치밀어, 메스꺼운
- **disappointment** 실망

- **sign** 흔적, 신호, 표시
- **agree** 동의하다, 찬성하다
- **not at all** 전혀 ~ 않다
- **should + 동사원형** ~해야 한다
- **a bit** 조금, 약간
- **even though** 비록 ~일지라도
- **increasingly** 갈수록 더
- **argumentative** 따지기 좋아하는, 시비를 거는
- **warily** 조심하여, 주의깊게

Aha! Science

섬은 어떻게 생기나요?

주위가 물에 완전히 둘러싸여 있는 육지를 섬이라고 해요. 섬은 지각운동으로 바닷속 땅 일부가 융기하거나, 해안산맥 일부가 물속으로 가라앉아 높은 땅 일부만 해수면 위에 남겨지거나, 육지 일부가 가라앉고 그곳에 해수가 침입하는 등의 현상으로 생겨요. 해저화산이 분출하거나 해안 지역 일부가 파도나 빙하의 침식을 받아서 육지에서 분리되어 이루어지는 경우도 있답니다.

At last, they spotted a sandy shore beyond the water. They
climbed up a small hill and Doniphan reached the top first.
"It's not the sea at all," he said. "It's a huge lake, which
means that we're not on an island, Briant."
Briant was still not sure about that, but he kept quiet for
now, since Gordon had asked him before they left to try not
to argue with Doniphan.
When they came back to the lake shore near the forest,
Phann began to behave strangely. He ran toward a group of
trees on the lake shore, barking and running back and forth
between the trees and the boys.
It seemed that he wanted the boys to follow him, so they did.
They found a tree with some letters and a year scratched on
it.

FB

1807

- **spot** 발견하다, 찾다; 장소
- **climb up** 오르다
- **keep quiet** 침묵을 지키다(keep-kept-kept)
- **since** ~ 때문에; ~이래 줄곧
- **argue** 언쟁하다, 주장하다
- **behave** (특정한 방식으로) 행동하다
- **strangely** 이상하게

- **a group of** 한 무리의
- **bark** (개가) 짖다; (개 등이) 짖는 소리
- **back and forth** 왔다 갔다
- **letter** 글자, 문자, 편지
- **scratch** 긁다, (긁어서 어떤 표시 등을) 그리다
  [없애다]; 찰과상

The boys looked at it thoughtfully, but as they were trying to figure out what it all meant, Phann hurried away again and disappeared.

They heard him barking again, and followed him to some bushes at the base of a cliff.

Behind the bushes, hidden by branches that had grown across it, was the entrance to a cave.

"Be careful," said Doniphan. "There could be something — or someone — living in there!"

"We must check that the air is good to breathe, too," warned Briant.

- **thoughtfully** 사려 깊이, 생각이 깊게
- **figure out** 알아내다, 이해하다
- **hurry away** 급히 가버리다
- **disappear** 사라지다(↔ appear 나타나다, ~처럼 보이다)
- **bush** 관목(키가 작고 줄기와 가지의 구별이 어렵고 가지를 많이 치는 나무), 덤불
- **base** 맨 아랫부분, 기초, 본부, (군사) 기지
- **hide** 감추다, 숨기다, 숨다(hide-hid-hidden)
- **branch** 나뭇가지
- **entrance** (출)입구, 등장
- **cave** 동굴
- **breathe** 호흡하다
- **warn** 경고하다

Aha! English

"We must check that the air is good to breathe, too." "우리는 그 공기가 호흡하기에 괜찮은지도 확인해야 해."

must는 보통 '~해야 하다'의 의미로 의무를 나타내는데 이때는 have to로 바꿔 쓸 수 있어요. 이 외에도 '~임에 틀림없다'라는 뜻으로도 쓰여요. 또한 must는 조동사이기 때문에 뒤에 동사원형이 와야 해요.

ex. You must go to hospital tomorrow. 너는 내일 반드시 병원에 가야 한다.

Tom must be tired after all that walking. 탐은 그렇게 걷고 나서 피곤할 것이 틀림없다.

The boys went into the cave, walking carefully and breathing
cautiously. The floor was dry and sandy, and the air was
good to breathe.
To their surprise, there was a table inside, with a tin cup and
a jug on it. There was even a clock on the wall, though it had
stopped telling the time long ago.

- **carefully** 조심스럽게, 신중히
- **cautiously** 조심스럽게, 신중하게
- **floor** 바닥, (건물의) 층
- **tin** (금속) 주석, 통조림 깡통
- **jug** 주전자, 단지
- **stop + 동사원형-ing** ~하는 것을 멈추다

It was clear to the boys that someone had lived here at some time, and it was hard to tell how long ago.

Outside, Phann was still barking.

The boys went out to see him and, to their horror, there was a skeleton lying on the bank of the river! 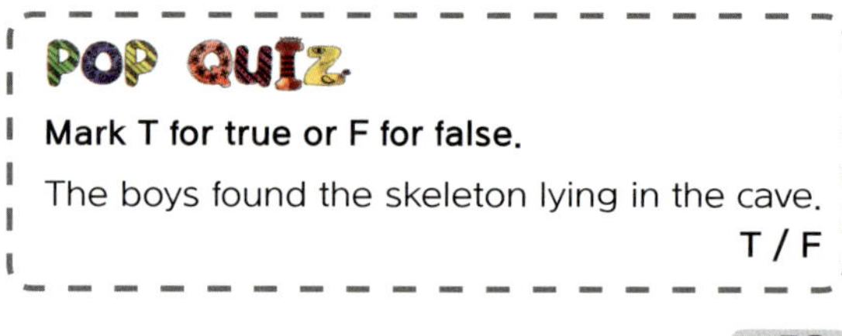 The boys were shocked at the sight.

This person must have been shipwrecked and must have lived in the cave, but the fact that his skeleton was still here meant that he had never managed to leave this place.

POP QUIZ

Mark T for true or F for false.

The boys found the skeleton lying in the cave.

T / F

정답 F

- **to one's horror** 두렵게도(*cf.* horror 공포, 전율)
- **skeleton** 해골, 뼈대
- **lie** 놓여 있다, 묻혀 있다, 눕다(lie-lay-lain)
- **bank** 강둑, 경사지, 은행
- **be shocked at** ~에 깜짝 놀라다
- **sight** 광경, 시력, 시야
- **shipwreck** (해상에서) 조난을 당하다; 난파, 조난 사고
- **fact** 사실
- **manage to + 동사원형** 간신히(어떻게 해서든) ~하다 [해내다]

Aha! English

~, there was a skeleton <u>lying</u> on the bank of the river! ~, 강둑에 <u>놓여 있는</u> 해골이 하나 있었다!

lie는 비슷한 모양을 지닌 다른 단어들과 헷갈릴 수 있어요. lie는 기본적으로 '눕다, 누워 있다, 놓여 있다'라는 뜻으로 쓰이며, 과거형과 과거분사는 lay-lain이에요. 또한 '거짓말하다'라는 뜻으로도 쓰이는데, 이때의 과거형과 과거분사는 lied-lied이니 주의해야 해요. 또 다른 비슷한 모양의 단어로는 lay(~을 두다(lay-laid-laid))가 있어요.

lie-lay-lain(눕다, 놓여 있다)　lie-lied-lied(거짓말하다)　lay-laid-laid(~을 두다)

Briant felt a chill at the thought, because it meant that the boys might never leave the island either.

Still, if this man could live in the cave, then they could live in the cave, too, until they came up with a better plan.

The cave was dry, and big enough for all the boys to live in.

- **feel a chill** 오싹해지다(feel-felt-felt)
- **thought** 생각
- **either** (부정문에서) ~도[또한]

- **come up with** 생각해내다, 제시하다 (come-came-come)
- **plan** 계획; 계획하다

When they went back inside for another search, they found a book with a lot of writing in it. The words were impossible to read, except a name: François Baudoin. FB: the same initials as those carved on the tree!

"The skeleton must be François Baudoin," said Briant.

Doniphan suddenly shouted, "I've found a map! It was hidden here between the pages of the book!"

"François must have drawn it," said Briant, leaning over Doniphan's shoulder to take a closer look.

It was a map of the whole area, proving that it really was an island.

"So you were right, Briant," said Doniphan, gloomily. "This place is an island and therefore we cannot leave here without a boat."

POP QUIZ

What did Doniphan find in the book?

ⓐ a map
ⓑ a letter

- **a lot of** 많은(= lots of)
- **writing** 글자, 글씨, 글
- **word** 단어, 낱말
- **impossible** 불가능한(↔ possible 가능한)
- **name** 이름; 이름을 짓다
- **initial** 단어의 첫 머리에 나오는 글자
- **carve** (글씨를) 새기다, 조각하다
- **lean over** ~ 너머로 몸을 구부리다
- **take a look** 살펴보다, 점검하다(= have a look)
- **area** 지역, 구역
- **gloomily** 우울하게, 어둡게
- **therefore** 그러므로

The boys dug a grave for François and said a prayer for his soul there. Then, they hurried back to tell Gordon about the cave.

On the way back, they got lost, even though they tried to use the map to find the way back.

Night fell, and they faced another night in the forest with no way of knowing where they were.

Then, in the silence of the night, there was a sudden bang and a flash of light. Gordon had sent up a flare from the boat to signal the way back! The boys hurried thankfully in the direction of the rocket and got back to the boat within an hour.

- **dig** 파다, 캐내다(dig-dug-dug)
- **grave** 무덤
- **say a prayer** 기도하다(*cf*. prayer 기도, 기도 내용)
- **soul** 영혼, 정신
- **on the way back** 돌아가는 길에
- **get lost** 길을 잃다
- **fall** (어둠·침묵 등이) 닥치다, 넘어지다(fall-fell-fallen)
- **face** 직면하다, 향하다; 얼굴, 표정
- **silence** 고요, 침묵
- **sudden** 갑작스러운
- **bang** 탕, 쾅, 툭 (소리); 쾅[탕] 하고 치다[닫다]
- **flash** 번쩍임; 비추다, (불빛으로) 신호를 보내다
- **flare** 조명탄; (잠깐 동안) 확 타오르다

- **signal** 신호를 보내다; 신호
- **thankfully** 다행스럽게도, 고맙게도
- **in the direction of** ~의 방향으로
- **rocket** (하늘 높이 쏘아 올리는) 불꽃, 폭죽
- **get back** 돌아오다
- **within** (특정한 기간) 이내에[안에]
- **French** 프랑스의; 프랑스인
- **build** 만들다, 짓다(build-built-built)
- **raft** 뗏목, 소형 고무[플라스틱] 보트
- **unusual** 특이한, 드문(↔ usual 보통의)
- **be known for** ~로 알려지다
- **confident** 자신감 있는

Everyone thought it was a good idea to go and live in the cave, which they called French Cave because a French man had lived there.

They built a raft to carry everything to the cave and they sailed it all the way along the river from the beach to the cave.

Everyone was very excited when they got there, except Briant's brother, Jack, who still seemed quiet and sad. It was very unusual for him, because he had always been known for being a happy and confident boy.

"You're hiding something," Briant whispered to Jack, "or are you ill?"

Jack just shook his head, but refused to say anything about it.

The boys brought in all the beds and tables from the boat, so they were nice and cozy in the cave.

Moko made a good meal and there was a party atmosphere in the cave that night.

As the days went on, the boys settled into life at French Cave.
Doniphan stirred up arguments all the time, but Gordon
managed to calm everything down.

He gave lessons from the books that he had brought from the
boat, and everyone sat and listened.

The boys made the cave bigger with their tools from the
boat.

Luckily, the rock was soft enough for them to chip away at it
and they soon dug it away.

They also made two narrow windows in the walls so that
they could look out through them and fresh air could flow
into the cave.

The boys were all safe despite floods and storms outside.

- **ill** 아픈
- **shake one's head** 고개를 가로젓다
  (shake-shook-shaken)
- **refuse** 거부하다
- **bring** 가져오다, 데리고 오다
  (bring-brought-brought)
- **cozy** 편안한, 아늑한
- **atmosphere** 분위기, 대기
- **go on** (시간이) 흐르다, 계속되다
- **settle into** 자리잡다, 정착하다
- **stir up** (강한 감정을) 불러일으키다, 유발하다

- **argument** 논쟁, 말다툼
- **all the time** 항상
- **calm ~ down** ~을 진정시키다, 진정하다
- **give lessons** 가르치다, 수업하다
- **tool** 기구, 도구
- **chip away** (~을) 조금씩 잘라내다
- **narrow** 좁은, 가는
- **fresh** 신선한
- **flow** (액체·기체·전류가) 흐르다; 흐름
- **despite** ~에도 불구하고(= in spite of)
- **flood** 홍수

Now that they had a bigger cave to live in, the boys decided to name the main parts of the island.

"Let us call it Chairman Island," suggested Gordon, "after the chairman of the board who runs our school. He arranged the voyage for us, so we shall name the island after him."

They named the beach where the boat was wrecked Schooner Bay, because a schooner was the type of boat they had sailed in. 

"We need a leader," said Briant, "and I think it should be you, Gordon."

Most boys agreed with Briant, so Gordon became the leader on Chairman Island.

- **now that** ~이기 때문에, ~이므로
- **main** 주요한
- **let** ~하게 하다[두다](let-let-let)
- **chairman** 의장, 회장
- **run a school** 학교를 경영하다
- **arrange** 마련하다, (일을) 처리하다, 배열하다
- **shall + 동사원형** ~일[할] 것이다
- **name after** ~의 이름을 따서 이름 짓다
- **schooner** 스쿠너(돛대가 두 개 이상인, 바람의 힘으로 항해하는 배)
- **bay** 만(바다가 육지 속으로 파고들어 와 있는 곳)
- **type** 유형, 종류
- **turn** (~한 상태로) 바뀌다, 돌다, 돌리다
- **bitterly** 몹시, 비통하게, 격렬히
- **deep** (아래로, 안으로) 깊은, (겨울 또는 밤이) 깊은
- **busy + 동사원형 -ing** ~하느라 바쁜
- **learn** 배우다
- **melt** 녹다[녹이다], 누그러지다
- **hunt** 사냥하다
- **be good at + 동사원형 -ing** ~에 능숙하다
- **particularly** 특히, 유난히
- **shoot** 쏘다(shoot-shot-shot)

Aha! Science

bay 만

바다가 육지쪽으로 들어와 있는 형태를 만(bay)이라고 해요. 멕시코 만과 같은 규모가 큰 것부터 소규모인 것까지 다양한데, 규모가 작은 것은 물결이 잔잔하여 풍랑 대피항이나 항구로 발달되어 있는 곳이 많아요. 반대로 육지가 바다에 길게 돌출하여 삼면이 바다로 둘러싸여 있는 것은 반도라고 해요.

Winter came and the weather turned bitterly cold. The snow was so deep that nobody could leave the cave.

Gordon kept everyone busy washing clothes and learning their lessons from the books.

When the snow melted, the boys went out and hunted for food. There were plenty of animals around the island, and Doniphan was particularly good at using the guns to shoot them.

Briant talked about building a boat so that they could leave the island, but Gordon liked living there and made more plans to keep everyone comfortable.

Gordon was a good leader, but Doniphan was jealous of him and Briant, so he began to complain about both of them. One day, he even got into a fight with Briant over a game. Gordon had to come and separate the two of them.

"Why should you be the leader, Gordon?" growled Doniphan. "I could be a better leader than you, and I think I should be the leader."

His friends, Wilcox and Webb, and his cousin, Cross, agreed
with him. They went around trying to persuade the other
boys that Doniphan should be the new leader.

Cross had always admired Doniphan and did everything that
his cousin said. Webb and Wilcox were only twelve, and
they were not particularly clever. They liked to quarrel with
one another and to persuade other people to do their work
for them.

These were the kind of boys that Doniphan gathered around
him — boys who would do what he told them without
questioning him.

Some of the other boys listened, and some ignored Doniphan
and his friends.

- **be jealous of** ~을 질투[시샘]하다
- **complain** 불평하다, 항의하다
- **get into a fight** 싸움을 시작하다
- **separate** 분리하다[분리되다]; 분리된
- **growl** 화난 목소리로 말하다, 으르렁거리다
- **go around** 돌아다니다
- **persuade** 설득하다, 납득시키다

- **admire** 존경하다, 칭찬하다
- **clever** 똑똑한, 영리한
- **quarrel** 다투다, 언쟁하다; 싸움
- **one another** 서로
- **the kind of** 이같은
- **ignore** 무시하다

Briant was still worried about his brother, Jack, who was becoming sadder and sadder.

At last, Jack spoke to Briant about his secret.

"You might forgive me," he said, "but I don't think the other boys will."

"But what have you done?" asked Briant.

"You will find out soon enough," said Jack, starting to cry.

The boys had gathered a few animals and birds by now.

They made some farm enclosures for them.

Moko cooked some wonderful food with eggs from the birds and milk from the vicuña, a creature like a llama.  He even managed to make a sugar syrup from the sap of a maple tree, so everyone ate well!

"I will go and explore the east side of the island," said Briant.

"Then, I can see if any ships pass on that side."

He took Moko and Jack with him. They sailed in a small boat that they had brought from the larger, wrecked boat.

POP QUIZ

What animal provided milk to the boys?

ⓐ a llama   ⓑ a vicuña

ⓑ 답정

- **sadder** 더 슬픈(sad의 비교급)
- **forgive** 용서하다(forgive-forgave-forgiven)
- **find out** 알아내다, 알게 되다
- **soon enough** 곧
- **enclosure** 울타리, (토지를) 둘러쌈, 동봉(물)
- **milk** 젖, 우유; 젖을 짜다
- **vicuña** 비쿠냐(털이 아주 부드러운 야생 라마의 일종)

- **creature** 동물, 생명체
- **llama** 라마(남미에서 털을 얻고 짐을 운반하게 하려고 기르는 가축)
- **sap** 수액
- **maple tree** 단풍나무
- **east** 동쪽의; 동쪽
- **pass** 지나가다, 건네주다, 합격하다

Aha! Science

vicuña 비쿠냐

우리에게 생소한 비쿠냐는 야생 라마의 한 종류예요. 머리는 작고, 목은 길며 털은 노란빛을 띤 갈색이에요. 목 아래쪽에서 앞가슴에 이르는 부분에 20~30cm의 희고 긴 털이 있답니다. 특이하게 한마리의 수컷을 중심으로 십여 마리의 암컷이 무리를 지어 생활해요. 비쿠냐의 털에서 채취한 섬유는 가늘고 광택이 풍부하며 모든 동물 섬유 중 가장 곱고 부드러운 섬유로 평가되고 있어요.

After a long journey along the river, they reached the eastern coast. There was a sandy beach with only a few rocks there, but no ships passed that way, even though they stayed watching all day.

Briant called the place Deception Bay because he felt as though the place had deceived him. He looked through his telescope and frowned as he saw something strange on the horizon. It looked like a cloud, but the sky was clear. Briant did not know what it was, even though Moko said that he could see it, too.

After a while, Briant and Jack went for a walk on their own, leaving Moko behind to wait for the tide to change so that they could sail their boat back to the cave.

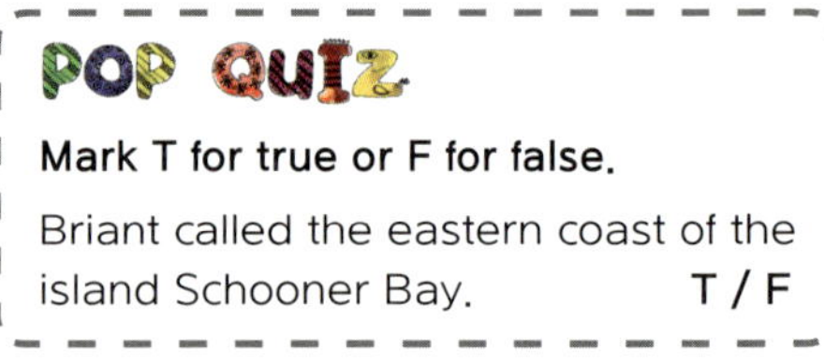

정답 F

- **journey** 여행, 여정
- **eastern** 동쪽의, 동쪽에 있는
- **coast** 해안
- **deception** 사기, 속임(수), 기만
- **deceive** 속이다
- **look through** (빠르게) 살펴보다
- **telescope** 망원경

- **frown** 얼굴을 찌푸리다; 찌푸림
- **go for a walk** 산책하러 가다
- **on one's own** 혼자서, 혼자 힘으로
- **leave ~ behind** ~을 두고 가다, ~을 둔 채 잊고 가다
- **wait for** 기다리다
- **tide** 밀물과 썰물, 조류(밀물과 썰물로 발생하는 바닷물의 흐름)

Moko couldn't help but overhear Briant and Jack talking about Jack's secret.

"You did it!" gasped Briant, his voice shocked.

"I'm sorry," said Jack, as he began to cry again.

"You must not tell the others," said Briant.

- **can't help but + 동사원형** ~하지 않을 수 없다
- **overhear** (말하는 사람이 모르게) 우연히 듣다, 엿듣다(overhear-overheard-overheard)
- **gasp** 숨이 턱 막히다

A 섬과 관련된 장소와 각 지명에 쓰인 단어를 올바르게 연결하세요.

❶ the bay on the east side of the island · · a) French

❷ the island · · b) Schooner

❸ the bay where the boat landed · · c) Chairman

❹ the cave · · d) Deception

B 빈칸에 알맞은 말을 골라 넣어 문장을 완성하세요.

shipwrecked	impossible	shocked	hidden

❶ The boys were __________ at the sight of the skeleton.

❷ The man, François Baudoin, must have been __________.

❸ The words in the book were __________ to read.

❹ The map was __________ in the pages of the book.

Answers

A ❶ d ❷ c ❸ b ❹ a
B ❶ shocked ❷ shipwrecked ❸ impossible ❹ hidden

 다음 질문에 알맞은 답을 고르세요.

❶ Why did NOT Jack want to tell anyone his secret?

a) He didn't think the other boys would forgive him.

b) He didn't think that Briant would forgive him.

c) He didn't think that anyone would want to hear it.

d) He didn't think that anyone would believe it.

❷ How did the boys carry everything from the boat to the cave?

a) They carried it on their backs.

b) They loaded it onto the backs of animals.

c) They made a cart and pulled it along.

d) They made a raft and sailed it along the river.

❸ What was NOT right about the cave?

a) The floor was dry.

b) There was a clock on the wall.

c) There was a skeleton in the corner.

d) There was a tin cup on the table.

Answers

C   ❶ a   ❷ d   ❸ c

Unwanted Visitors

원치 않은 방문객들

When Briant, Jack, and Moko got back to the cave, life went on as usual.

Doniphan kept arguing with everyone and he complained about everything.

By now, Gordon had been the leader of the island for a whole year.

"It's time to elect a new leader," said Doniphan, who hoped that he would be elected as the new leader.

But Briant was elected instead, and all through another winter, Doniphan grew angrier and angrier.

- **unwanted** 원치 않은[는], 반갑지 않은
- **visitor** 방문객
- **as usual** 평상시처럼
- **keep + 동사원형-ing** 계속해서 ~하다
- **it's time to + 동사원형** ~할 시간이다
- **elect** (선거로) 선출하다

- **angrier** 더 화가 난(angry의 비교급)
  (*cf*.비교급 + and + 비교급: 점점 더 ~한/~하게)
- **no longer** 더 이상 ~ 않다
- **be tired of** ~에 신물[싫증]이 나다
- **snap at** ~에게 쏘아붙이다, ~에 달려들다
- **perfectly** 완벽하게

When summer came again, Doniphan could stand it no longer.

"I'm tired of doing what you say," he snapped at Briant, and he took Cross, Wilcox, and Webb away to Deception Bay.

"We don't need the others," he said. "We can live perfectly well here on our own."

The first night at Deception Bay was very stormy, with crashing thunder and flashing lightning. 

As Doniphan and his friends sheltered in the forest at the edge of the beach, Wilcox noticed something strange.

"What's that?" he shouted, pointing at a large, dark shape on the beach.

It looked like a boat. The boys rushed out to have a look, and found that it was a boat.

ⓑ 답정

- **stormy** 폭풍우 치는
- **thunder** 천둥
- **flash** 번쩍이다, 비치다
- **lightning** 번개
- **at the edge of** ~의 끝[가장자리]에서

- **point** (손가락 등으로) 가리키다, 겨누다; (말이나 글에서 제시하는) 주장
- **shape** 형태, 모양
- **rush** 돌진하다, 서두르다, 재촉하다

Aha! Science

번개는 빛, 천둥은 소리?

천둥과 번개는 함께 발생해요. 격렬하게 움직이는 대기 속에서 얼음 알갱이들은 서로 부딪히면서 정전기를 만들어 내요. 이때 아래쪽에는 음전하가, 위쪽에는 양전하가 몰리는데, 서로 다른 전하(물체가 띠고 있는 정전기의 양)가 부딪혀서 엄청난 에너지의 불꽃을 만들어 내는 것을 번개라고 해요. 즉, 하늘과 땅 사이의 전위차에 따른 방전으로 인해 번개가 발생해요. 천둥은 번개가 나타날 때 같이 발생하는 소리를 말해요. 소리의 속도는 빛의 속도보다 느리기 때문에, 번개의 불꽃을 본 뒤에 천둥소리를 듣게 되죠.

Two bodies lay next to it on the sand. The boys thought that they should stay and try to help, but the storm was so fierce that they were too afraid. They hurried back to the shelter of the trees.

During the night, they thought they heard distant cries, but when the lightning stopped, it was too dark to see anything.

■ **next to** ~ 바로 옆에, ~ 다음의   ■ **fierce** 사나운, 격렬한, 격심한   ■ **distant** 먼, (멀리) 떨어져 있는

In the morning, when it was light, the boys went to the boat to have a look. But the two bodies had disappeared, and there was no sign that they had been dragged away by wild animals.

"The tide must have washed them away," said Doniphan.

The boat was smashed on one side, but at the back they could still read a name: "Severn".

The words "San Francisco" were also written on it, indicating the port from which it had sailed.

"It's come from America," said Doniphan. "I wonder if that means that we are close to the coast of America."

- **drag** (힘들여) 끌다[끌고 가다]
- **smash** 박살나다, 박살내다, 부딪치다
- **San Francisco** 샌프란시스코(미국의 도시)
- **indicate** 나타내다, 가리키다

- **port** 항구, 항만
- **America** 미국, 아메리카 대륙
- **wonder** 궁금하다, ~이 아닐까 생각하다
- **be close to** ~에서 가깝다

Aha! Culture

San Francisco 샌프란시스코

샌프란시스코는 미국 캘리포니아주(州) 서부에 있는 세계적인 항구 도시예요. 1850년대 시에라네바다 산지에서 금광맥이 발견되어, 골드러시 시대를 맞으며 도시가 본격적으로 발전하기 시작했어요. 1869년 첫 번째 대륙횡단철도가 완성되면서 미국 서부의 성장 중심지가 되었을 뿐만 아니라 태평양 국가들과의 상업 교류를 위한 주요 위치를 점하게 되었어요. 태평양을 접하고 있어 해양성 기후로 연중 온화한 날씨가 지속된답니다.

Severn,
San Francisco

Back at French Cave, everyone was sad. They wished that
Doniphan and his friends had not gone away.
But there were other things to think about, such as the need
for a signal in case any boats passed by the island.
"Let's make a kite," suggested Briant. "It will go high into
the sky and if any ships pass, they will see it."
The younger boys were very excited about Briant's idea and
they had a wonderful time making a huge kite.

▲ 윈치

They attached it to the heavy metal winch from the boat. They anchored it to the ground so that it could not float away.

Just as the boys got ready to launch the kite, Phann went toward the forest, barking yet again.

"What has he found this time?" asked Gordon, as all the boys followed the dog.

This time, Phann led them to a woman, who was lying under a tree, unconscious but alive. They took her back to the cave and wet her lips with some brandy.

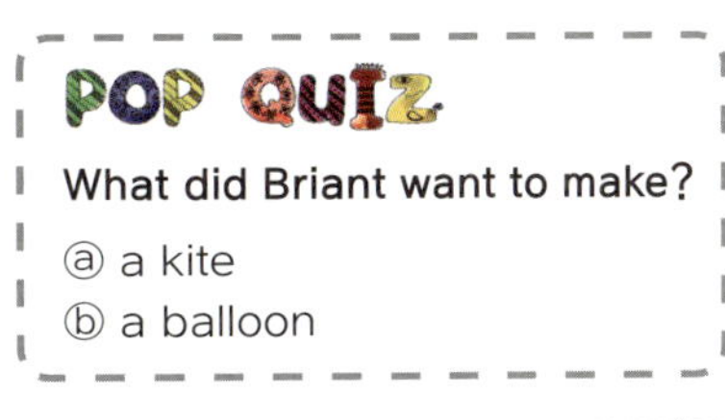

ⓔ 답정

- **go away** (사람·장소를) 떠나가다, 없어지다
- **pass by** (~을) 지나가다
- **kite** 연(공중에 높이 날리는 장난감)
- **attach** 부착하다, 달다, 첨부하다, 애착을 갖다
- **metal** 금속
- **winch** 윈치(선박에 설치된 기계로 짐을 오르내리게 하거나 이동시킴)
- **anchor** 고정시키다, 닻을 내리다, 정박하다; 닻

- **float away** 둥둥 떠가다
- **get ready to + 동사원형** ~할 준비가 되다
- **launch** (비행기 등을) 날리다, 발사하다, 개시하다, 출시하다
- **unconscious** 의식을 잃은, 무의식의
- **alive** 살아 있는
- **wet** 적시다; 젖은
- **brandy** 브랜디(과실주를 증류한 술)

When the woman, who appeared to be in her forties, woke
up, she told them her story.

"My name is Kate," she said. "I was a servant in America
when my employer and his wife took me on a voyage to
Chile in a boat called the 'Severn'."

Kate told the boys all about the crew of the "Severn." They
had killed the captain, Kate's employer, and his wife so that
they could take charge of the boat and everything on it.

- **in one's forties** 40대에
- **employer** 고용주(↔ employee 고용인)

- **Chile** 칠레
- **take charge of** 주도권을 잡다, ~을 떠맡다, 돌보다

Their leader was called Walston and most of the others were mostly bad men. They did what Walston told them to do, although one of them, called Forbes, was less cruel than the others. He persuaded them to spare Kate's life.
The men also spared the life of the ship's master, Evans, who was second in command to the captain. They needed him to navigate.

- **mostly** 대부분, 주로, 거의
- **less** 더 적은[덜한]
- **cruel** 잔인한, 끔찍한, 엄한
- **spare** (남들은 피할 수 없었던 상해·죽음 등을) 피하게 해주다
- **master** 주인
- **second in command** 2인자, 부사령관
- **navigate** 항해하다, 길을 찾다

Kate told the boys how the boat had caught fire and one man had died when he jumped overboard to escape from the flames.

Nobody knew how the fire had started, but it was so fierce that the entire ship burned up and sank.

Luckily, there was a lifeboat which they had jumped into. This was the boat that had washed ashore on Chairman Island, with the crew and Kate aboard.

Kate was thrown onto the beach when the lifeboat landed, and after a while she managed to get up and escape without being seen. The men probably thought that she was dead by now.

- **catch fire** 불이 붙다(catch-caught-caught)
- **overboard** 배 밖으로, (배 밖의) 물속으로
- **escape** 탈출하다
- **flame** 불길; 활활 타오르다
- **entire** 전체의
- **burn up** 전소되다, 모두 태우다
- **lifeboat** 구명보트, 구명정
- **be thrown onto** ~ 위로 던져지다
  (*cf.* throw 던지다(throw-threw-thrown))
- **probably** 아마도
- **dead** 죽은

Aha! English

~, but it was so fierce that the entire ship burned up and sank. ~, 그러나 그것은 너무 맹렬해서 배 전체가 완전히 불타고 가라앉았다.

'so + 형용사/부사 + that + 주어 + 동사'는 '너무 …해서 ~하다'라는 뜻으로 원인과 결과를 나타내요. 그런데 이 so that을 서로 붙여서 사용하면 뜻이 달라져요. I walk every morning so that I can stay healthy. (나는 건강하게 지내기 위해 매일 아침 걷는다.)처럼 '…하기 위해 ~하다'라는 뜻으로 쓰여요.

ex. Tom was so rude that his mother got angry. 톰이 너무 무례해서 그의 엄마는 화가 났다.

Briant was horrified to hear that there were dangerous men on the island!

"We must find Doniphan and the others," he cried. "We will bring them back to the cave where they will be safer."

He and Moko set out to look for them, taking the boat along the river and into the deep, dark forest.

- **horrified** 공포에 휩싸인, 충격을 받은
- **dangerous** 위험한

- **look for** ~을 찾다

Doniphan and his friends were camping in the forest, next to a flickering fire.

A jaguar attacked Doniphan just at the moment that Briant and Moko arrived. 

Wilcox grabbed his gun to shoot the jaguar, but Briant shouted, "Don't shoot!"

He slashed at the jaguar with his knife, injuring his shoulder as he did so.

The jaguar limped away, giving the boys a chance to escape.

"Come on!" gasped Briant, clutching his shoulder. "Let's go!"

"Thank you for saving my life," said Doniphan.

- **flickering** 꺼질 것 같은, 깜박거리는
  (*cf*. flicker (전깃불이나 불길이) 깜박거리다)
- **jaguar** (동물) 재규어
- **attack** 공격하다; 공격
- **moment** (특정한) 순간, 때
- **arrive** 도착하다
- **grab** 붙잡다, 움켜잡다
- **slash** (칼 등으로) 베다, 베어 상처를 내다, 매질하다
- **injure** 상처를 입히다, 손상하다
- **limp** 절뚝거리다, 불안정하게 움직이다
- **chance** 기회, 가능성
- **Come on!** 서둘러!, 어서!
- **clutch** 꽉 움켜잡다
- **save one's life** 생명을 구하다
- **thank you for ~** ~에 대해 감사하다

Aha! Science

jaguar 재규어

표범과 비슷해 보이는 재규어는 먹이 사슬의 최상위 층에 위치하며, 물가나 늪지가 가까운 밀림에 주로 살아요. 표범과 달리 얼룩무늬 중앙에 검은 점이 있으며 표범보다 몸이 훨씬 크고 억세게 생겼어요. 단독 생활을 하며 헤엄을 잘 치고 나무도 잘 탄답니다. 육식동물로 사슴, 소뿐만 아니라 껍질이 딱딱한 파충류도 잡아먹어요.

Briant led them back to the boat, telling them about the dangerous men on the way.

"That is why I told you not to shoot, Wilcox," he explained. "The men might hear the shot and then they would know that they are not alone on the island."

Friends once more, Briant and Doniphan sailed the boat back to the cave and all fifteen boys were reunited.

Everyone had to be very careful not to be discovered. Briant did not allow them to go far from the cave in case the dangerous men found them.

POP QUIZ

Mark T for true or F for false.

Friends once more, Briant and Doniphan sailed the boat back to the wrecked boat.   T / F

정답 F

- **explain** 설명하다
- **alone** 혼자, 홀로
- **once more** 한 번 더, 다시 한 번
- **reunite** 다시 통합[결합]시키다
- **allow A to B** A가 B 하는 것을 허락하다[용납하다]
- **crazy** 굉장히 좋은, 미친
- **be able to + 동사원형** ~할 수 있다(= can)

- **exactly** 정확히
- **calculate** 계산하다
- **how to + 동사원형** ~하는 방법
- **support** 지지하다, 후원하다
- **weight** 무게
- **hang** 매달다, 늘어뜨리다(hang-hung-hung)
- **beneath** ~ 아래[밑]에

Then, Briant had a crazy idea.

"We can send this kite high into the air," he said. "A boy can go up with it. He will be able to see the whole island and will be able to see exactly where the men are."

The other boys agreed that this might be possible. They spent several days calculating how to support the weight of a boy, yet still allow the kite to fly. They made a basket to hang beneath the kite, so a boy could stand in it.

"Who will go up in it?" asked Gordon.

Jack volunteered, but so did Doniphan and some of the other boys.

"I must do it," insisted Jack, "because I want to make up for the wrong thing I did."

At last, he confessed that it was he who had untied the rope in the harbor in Auckland. It was his fault that the boat had sailed away.

"It was meant to be a joke," he said in a small, sorry voice.

"Don't worry," said Doniphan. "It was a mistake and we will forgive you."

Now everyone realized why Jack had been so sad all this time.

They all agreed that he could go up in the basket to view the island. But Briant didn't want his younger brother to do something so dangerous. So, when Jack was about to step into the basket, Briant jumped in first and gave the order to launch!

- **volunteer** 자원하다, 자원봉사 하다; 자원봉사자
- **insist** 고집하다, 주장하다
- **make up for** 만회하다, 보상하다
- **wrong** 잘못된
- **confess** (죄·과실 등을) 자백하다, 고백하다
- **Auckland** 오클랜드(뉴질랜드 북섬에 있는 도시)
- **fault** 잘못, 책임, 결점
- **be meant to + 동사원형** ~ 하기로 되어 있다
- **joke** 장난, 농담

- **mistake** 실수; 실수하다
- **realize** 알아차리다, 실현하다
- **all this time** 지금껏 내내
- **view** 보다, ~라고 여기다; 시야, 견해
- **be about to + 동사원형** 막 ~하려 하다, ~하려는 참이다
- **step** (발걸음을 떼어) 움직이다, 서다; 걸음, 단계
- **order** 명령, 주문; 명령[주문]하다

🌐 Aha! Culture

뉴질랜드의 항구 도시, 오클랜드(Auckland)

오클랜드(Auckland)는 뉴질랜드 북섬에 있는 도시로 1865년까지 뉴질랜드의 수도였어요. 기후가 온난하여 태평양에서의 해상·항공 교통의 중심이며, 부근에 온천, 호수, 화산지형 등 관광자원이 많아요. 또한, 인근 섬들로의 선상 여행이 활발히 이루어지며 수상 스키와 윈드 서핑 등의 다양한 해양 스포츠도 유명해요. 오클랜드는 수도를 웰링턴으로 옮긴 뒤에도 꾸준히 번영했어요.

Comprehension Quiz

A 등장인물과 각 설명을 올바르게 연결하여 문장을 완성하세요.

❶ Kate •   • a) was the leader of the crew who took over the "Severn."

❷ Forbes •   • b) was thrown onto the beach when the lifeboat of the "Severn" landed.

❸ Walston •   • c) was less cruel than the other bad men on the crew of the "Severn."

B 빈칸에 알맞을 말을 골라 넣어 문장을 완성하세요.

basket	sad	kite	weight

❶ The other boys agreed that it might be possible to send a __________ high into the air.

❷ The boys spent several days calculating how a kite could support the __________ of a boy.

❸ The boys made a __________ to hang beneath the kite, so a boy could stand in it.

❹ Now everyone realized why Jack had been so __________ all this time.

Answers

A ❶ b   ❷ c   ❸ a
B ❶ kite   ❷ weight   ❸ basket   ❹ sad

 다음 질문에 알맞은 답을 고르세요.

❶ Why was everyone who left at the cave sad?

a) They wanted to go home to New Zealand.

b) Their cave had flooded during the storm.

c) They had lost their dog, Phann.

d) They wished that Doniphan and his friends had not gone away.

❷ Why did Briant want to make a kite?

a) just for fun

b) to act as a signal to passing ships

c) to teach the younger boys about engineering

d) to see which way the wind was blowing

❸ Why did Briant tell Wilcox NOT to shoot the jaguar?

a) He thought that the jaguar might attack Wilcox.

b) He wanted the jaguar to kill Doniphan.

c) He didn't want the jaguar to get hurt.

d) He didn't want the bad men to hear the sound of a gunshot.

Answers

C ❶ d   ❷ b   ❸ d

Chapter Four

Gun Battles
and Goodbyes

총격전 그리고 작별 인사

Briant and the kite went up and up into the night sky, soon disappearing into the shadows.

A rope was tied to the kite so that it couldn't float away on its own.

Briant went up for ten minutes, until the rope pulled tight and he hovered above the island in the breeze. He had a great view of everything below.

The first thing he saw was the glow of a fire in the east, but it was too far away to be on the island.

POP QUIZ

When did Briant go up in the kite?
ⓐ during the night
ⓑ during the day

- **gun battle** 총격전(cf. battle 전쟁)
- **shadow** 어둠, 그림자
- **hover** (허공을) 맴돌다, 머물다
- **breeze** 산들바람, 미풍
- **glow** 불빛; 빛나다, 타다
- **volcano** 화산
- **perhaps** 아마도
- **remember** 기억하다
- **glacier** 빙하

"Is it a volcano?" he wondered. "Perhaps there is land over there!"

He remembered the white spot he had seen from Deception Bay and thought that perhaps there was an island with a glacier on it.

Then, he spotted another fire, much closer this time. It showed Briant that the men were still on Chairman Island. He pulled on the rope to tell the others that they could bring him and the kite back down to earth.

But, as the kite was lowered, there was a sudden gust of wind. It was strong enough to break the rope and knock Briant out of the basket!

Everyone screamed his name as he fell through the air, but luckily he landed in the lake and swam to the shore, unhurt. The kite, without his weight to hold it down, floated away into the sky like a gigantic bird.

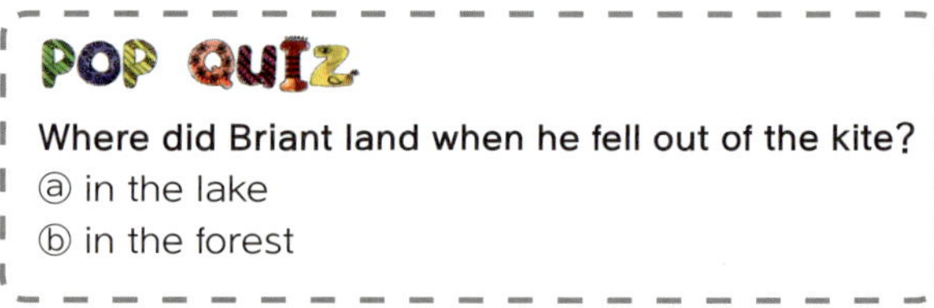

- **show** (~을 분명히) 보여 주다[증명하다], (특정한 정보를) 보여 주다
- **earth** 땅, 지면(*cf.* (the) Earth 지구)
- **lower** 내리다, 낮추다
- **gust** 세찬 바람, 돌풍, 갑작스런 분출
- **knock out of** ~에서 제거하다
- **unhurt** 손상되지 않은, 다치지 않은
- **gigantic** 거대한, 거인 같은
- **sound like** ~처럼 들리다
- **thrilled** (너무 좋아서) 황홀해 하는, 아주 흥분한
- **after all** 결국
- **mend** 수리하다, 바로잡다, 낫다

One stormy night, the boys and Kate were in the cave when they heard a voice outside, calling for help.

"It sounds like Evans," said Kate. "He is a good man, so it's safe to let him see us."

So the boys allowed Evans to come into the cave. He was thrilled to discover that Kate was alive after all.

"The lifeboat from the 'Severn' could be mended," he said, "but the men have no tools to do it, which is why they are still here."

"But we have tools," said Doniphan. "We could mend it!"

Evans told them that the dangerous men had found the
kite, which had landed on the island. Then, they knew that
someone else was on the island and soon after, they had
discovered the cave.

They were planning an attack to take over the cave and steal
everything in it.

Evans also told them that there was land nearby, so Briant
had been right!

"This island is near the coast of South America," he said, "and
its real name is Hanover Island."

So the boys began to make a plan to mend the lifeboat
with their tools, if only they could get to it without the men
stopping them. Then, they could sail away and perhaps find
a way back home.

But first, they had to deal with the men, which was not
going to be an easy task.

- **soon after** 곧, 얼마 지나지 않아
- **take over** 차지하다, 넘겨받다
- **steal** 훔치다(steal-stole-stolen)
- **South America** 남아메리카 대륙(*cf.* south 남쪽의; 남쪽)

- **if only** ~이면 좋을텐데
- **get to** ~에 도착하다, ~을 괴롭히다
- **deal with** ~을 (상)대하다, ~을 처리하다
- **task** 임무

One evening, the bad men's attack began in a strangely quiet way, when two men came to the cave. They pretended to be shipwrecked sailors and said that their names were Forbes and Rock.

"Will you help us," Forbes cried, "by giving us food and shelter?"

The boys brought the men into the cave, pretending to believe their story. They wanted to capture the men.

- **pretend** ~인 척하다
- **believe** 믿다, 확신하다
- **capture** 포로로 잡다, 포획하다

Once the men were in the cave, the boys pushed them into a storeroom and kept them prisoner there. The men tried to escape, but Evans grabbed Forbes. Unfortunately, Rock escaped and ran away, back to the other men.

ⓐ 답정

- **storeroom** 창고(*cf.* store 창고; 저장하다)
- **keep ~ prisoner** ~을 포로로 잡아두다
- **unfortunately** 불행하게도, 유감스럽게도
- **run away** 도망치다, 떠나다

Aha! English

The boys brought the men into the cave, pretending to believe their story. 소년들은 그 사내들의 이야기를 믿는 척하며 그들을 동굴로 들어오게 했다.

위 문장에서는 두 가지 동작(상황)이 거의 동시에 일어나고 있어요. pretending to believe their story는 While the boys pretend to believe their story를 분사를 이용해 축약해서 간단하게 표현한 것이에요. 이런 구문을 '분사구문'이라고 해요.

ex. Eating hamburger, I watched my favorite movie. 나는 햄버거를 먹으면서, 내가 가장 좋아하는 영화를 봤다.

The next day, there was the sound of gunshots, announcing the arrival of the other men.

The older boys rushed out of the cave and a great battle broke out.

There was a lot of fighting with guns and swords, and poor Doniphan was stabbed with a knife. He looked as though he might die.

"Get him back to the cave," shouted Gordon, but some of the men had already entered the cave.

Walston, the leader of the dangerous men, grabbed Jack.

He tried to take Jack away on the boys' boat, which was moored on the river near the cave.

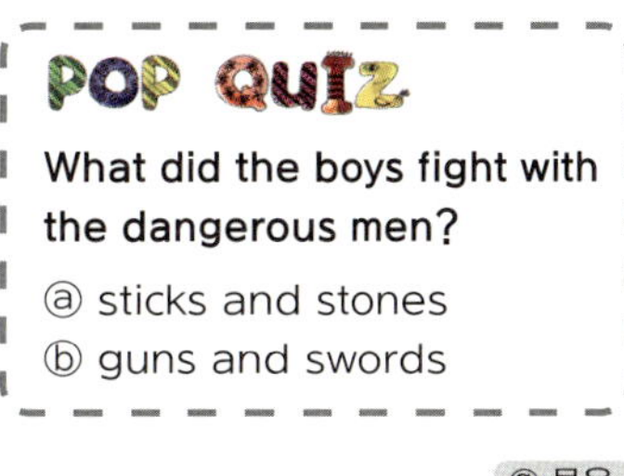

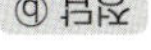

- **gunshot** 총소리, 발사
- **announce** 알리다, 발표하다
- **arrival** 도착
- **break out** 발발[발생]하다
- **fighting** 싸움, 전투
- **sword** (무기로 쓰이는 긴) 칼

- **poor** 불쌍한, 가난한
- **stab** (칼같이 뾰족한 것으로) 찌르다, 삿대질하다; 찌르기, 찔린 상처
- **enter** 들어가다, 입학하다, 시작하다
- **moor** 정박시키다

Forbes rushed out of the cave and attacked Walston, but was killed in the struggle. 

Everything seemed to be going wrong for the boys when something unexpected happened.

Moko had been hiding in a storeroom inside the cave, and remained undiscovered by the men.

Now, he came out of the storeroom with a gun. He fired some shots out through the windows of the cave.

Some of the men were killed and others were wounded.

They escaped into the forest, but died there of their wounds.

The boys knew this because Phann led them to the bodies.

The boys had won the battle, but Doniphan was seriously ill.

Kate dressed his wound with leaves and looked after him

through days and nights of pain and fever.

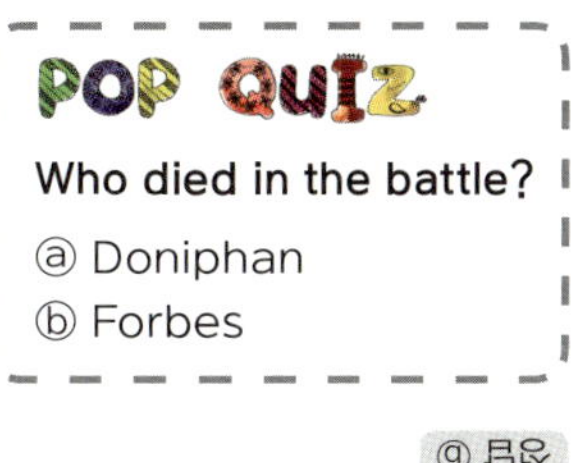

ⓑ 음양

- **struggle** 싸움, 힘든 일; 싸우다
- **go wrong** (일이) 잘못되다
- **unexpected** 예기치 못한
- **happen** (사건이) 발생하다
- **remain** 여전히 ~이다, 남다
- **undiscovered** 발견되지 않은
- **wounded** 부상당한, 다친

- **die of** ~로 죽다
- **wound** 부상, 상처
- **seriously** 심각하게
- **dress** (상처를) 치료하다, 옷을 입다[입히다]
- **day and night** 밤낮으로, 끊임없이
- **pain** 고통, 아픔
- **fever** 열, 열병

📖 Aha! English

Forbes rushed out of the cave ~ but was killed in the struggle. 포브스가 재빨리 동굴 밖으로 뛰쳐나가 ~, 하지만 싸우다가 <u>죽임을 당했다</u>.

주어가 어떤 행동을 '하는' 것이 아닌 '당하는' 상태를 나타낼 때는 'be + 과거분사(p.p.)' 형태로 써요. 위 문장에서 포브스는 죽이는 것이 아닌 '죽임을 당한' 상황이라 was killed로 쓰였어요.

ex. The food <u>is stored</u> in the cave. 식량은 동굴에 <u>저장되어</u> 있다.

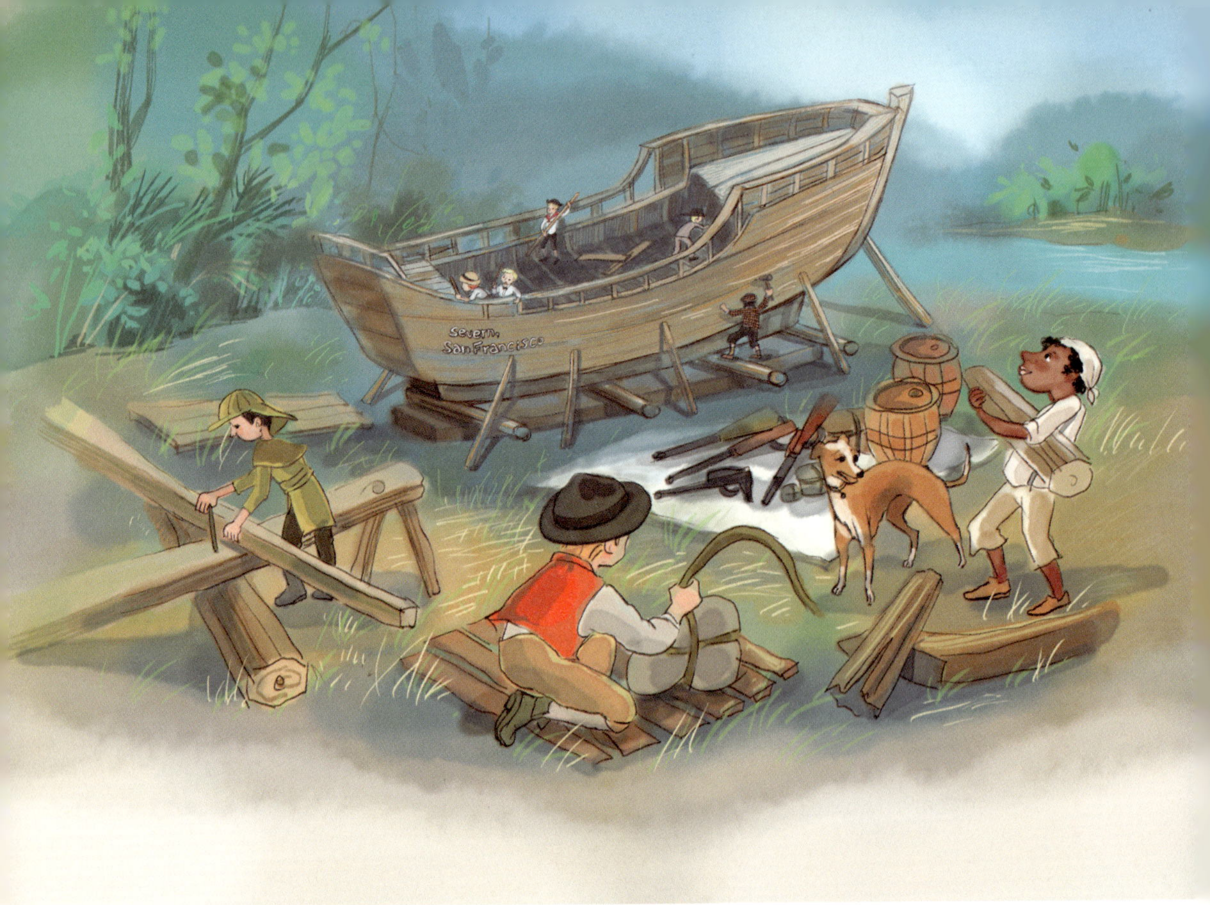

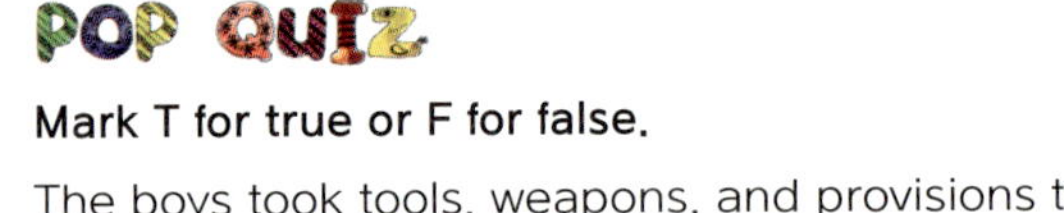

Meanwhile, the boys took tools, weapons, and provisions to Deception Bay.

They were ready to repair the lifeboat from the "Severn."

They worked hard on the repairs and, at last, the boat was ready.

POP QUIZ

Mark T for true or F for false.

The boys took tools, weapons, and provisions to French Cave to repair the lifeboat. T / F

정답 F

Thanks to Kate's careful nursing, Doniphan was getting better and, after a while, he was well enough to come to Deception Bay to join the others. 

After almost two years on the island, it was time to try and go home!

Before they left, the boys dug a grave for Forbes next to François Boudoin's grave. They said some prayers by the graves and thought for a while about these brave men.

ⓔ 月요

- **meanwhile** 한편, 그동안에
- **weapon** 무기
- **provisions** 식량, 양식
- **be ready to + 동사원형** ~할 준비가 되다
- **repair** 수리하다; 수리

- **hard** 열심히; 딱딱한, 여려운
- **thanks to** ~ 덕분에, ~에 힘입어, ~ 때문에
- **nursing** 간호, 돌봄(*cf.* nurse 간호하다; 간호사)
- **get better** 회복하다
- **for a while** 잠시 동안, 잠깐

Aha! English

~, he was well enough to come to Deception Bay to join the others. ~, 그는 다른 아이들과 합류하기 위해 사기 만으로 찾아올 만큼 충분히 건강해졌다.

'형용사 + enough to + 동사원형'은 '~할 만큼 충분히 …한'이라는 뜻이에요.

ex. The cave was dry, and big enough for all the boys to live in. 동굴은 건조했고, 모든 소년이 살 수 있을 만큼 충분히 컸다.

On the 5th February, the boys boarded the lifeboat, taking Kate and Evans with them. Even Phann stood proudly at the front of the boat as they departed.

After several days at sea, a steam ship picked them up and took them toward New Zealand, where their voyage had first begun.

On the 25th February, 1862, they finally arrived back in Auckland.

Their families had lost hope of seeing them alive and were overjoyed to see them.

"It's more than two years since we left," laughed Briant. "What a vacation we've had!"

- **February** 2월
- **proudly** 자랑스럽게
- **at the front of** ~의 앞부분에
- **depart** 출발하다, 떠나다
- **at sea** 해상에서, 항해 중인

- **pick up** ~을 찾다[발견하다]
- **lose** 잃다, 상실하다(lose-lost-lost)
- **overjoyed** 매우 기뻐하는
- **more than** ~ 이상의, ~보다 많이

A 등장인물과 각 설명을 올바르게 연결하여 문장을 완성하세요.

❶ Walston ·

· a) fired some shots out through the windows of the cave.

❷ Forbes ·

· b) ordered the boys to take Doniphan to the cave.

❸ Moko ·

· c) tried to take Jack away on the boat.

❹ Gordon ·

· d) rushed out of the cave but was killed in a struggle.

B 다음 내용이 옳으면 T, 틀리면 F에 표시하세요.

❶ The boys wanted to capture Forbes and Rock in a storeroom in the cave. T F

❷ Evans managed to escape from the cave. T F

❸ Doniphan was stabbed with a knife in the battle. T F

❹ Moko hid in a storeroom inside the cave during the battle. T F

Answers

A ❶ c ❷ d ❸ a ❹ b
B ❶ T ❷ F ❸ T ❹ T

 다음 질문에 알맞은 답을 고르세요.

❶ How did the dangerous men know that the boys were on the island?

a) They had seen the boys' footprints.

b) They had heard the boys' voices.

c) They had found the boys' kite.

d) They had found the boys' boat.

❷ How did Briant describe their experience on the island?

a) a vacation　　　　　　b) an adventure

c) a challenge　　　　　　d) a nightmare

D 이야기의 전개에 맞게 다음 문장들을 다시 배열하세요.

❶ The boys arrived back in Auckland.

❷ The boys said some prayers by the graves.

❸ A steam ship took them toward New Zealand.

❹ Everyone got into the lifeboat and set out to sea.

______ → ______ → ______ → ______

Answers

C　❶ c　　❷ a

D　❷ → ❹ → ❸ → ❶

Let's Review the Story

빈칸을 채우며 이야기를 다시 정리해 보세요.

Title: ___________ in the Pacific

Chapter 1:

Problem
- F_______ boys are ready to go on a voyage. The boat is accidentally cast adrift on the stormy P______ O______.

Solution
- The boat runs aground and the boys are on dry land again.

Chapter 2:

Problem
- The boys need to find f______ and a warm s______ as winter approaches.

Solution
- They find plenty to eat. Some of the boys e______ the i______ and Phann, the dog, leads the boys to a cave that they can live in.

Chapter 3:

Problem
- D______ and some of his friends l______ the others to live on their own. Some d______ men land on the island in a damaged lifeboat.

Solution
- B______ finds Doniphan, warns him, and brings the boys back to the c______. Everyone stays in the cave so that the men will not find them.

Chapter 4:

Problem
- The men a______ the c______, wounding Doniphan.

Solution
- The boys fight back with the help of Kate and Evans. They m______ the l______. Doniphan recovers, and they all sail away. They arrive home more than t______ years after they had left.

Let's Think & Talk

아래의 물음에 대해 생각해 보고 자유롭게 답하세요.

❶ 어른들 없이 친구들끼리만 2년 동안 무인도에서 지내야 한다면, 어떤 점이 즐겁고 어떤 점이 힘들 것 같나요? 또 어떤 규칙들이 필요할까요?

❷ 여러분이 만약 자크의 친구라면, 배를 바다로 흘러가게 한 장본인이 자크라는 것을 알았을 때 그를 어떻게 대할 것 같나요?

❸ 2년 동안 무인도에서 생활해야 한다면, 가장 가져가고 싶은 물건은 무엇인가요? 그 이유를 말해 보세요.

❹ 예상치 못했던 위기에 처했던 적이 있나요? 그 위기를 극복하기 위해 어떻게 했나요? 어떤 점이 가장 어려웠고, 어떻게 그 어려움을 이겨냈는지 이야기해 보세요.

Let's Review the Story

Title: Adrift in the Pacific

Chapter 1:

Problem
- Fifteen boys are ready to go on a voyage. The boat is accidentally cast adrift on the stormy Pacific Ocean .

Solution
- The boat runs aground and the boys are on dry land again.

Chapter 2:

Problem
- The boys need to find food and a warm shelter as winter approaches.

Solution
- They find plenty to eat. Some of the boys explore the island and Phann, the dog, leads the boys to a cave that they can live in.

Chapter 3:

Problem
- Doniphan and some of his friends leave the others to live on their own. Some dangerous men land on the island in a damaged lifeboat.

Solution
- Briant finds Doniphan, warns him, and brings the boys back to the cave . Everyone stays in the cave so that the men will not find them.

Chapter 4:

Problem
- The men attack the cave , wounding Doniphan.

Solution
- The boys fight back with the help of Kate and Evans. They mend the lifeboat . Doniphan recovers, and they all sail away. They arrive home more than two years after they had left.

Adrift in the Pacific

전문 번역

15소년 표류기

Adrift in the Pacific

p.10~11

1859년 말 뉴질랜드의 여름 방학이었고, 열네 명의 소년은 모두 매우 들떠 있었다. 그들은 모두 부유한 집 아들들을 위한 뉴질랜드의 한 학교에 재학 중이었고, 바다 여행을 가도록 선발되었다. 그들은 그들의 교육을 향상시키기 위해 뉴질랜드 전체를 항해할 예정이었다.

그 여행은 6주가 걸릴 것으로 예상되었다. 소년들은 방학을 보낼 더 좋은 방법을 생각할 수 없었다! 배에는 일곱 명의 선원이 있었다. 또한, 조리사와 모코라는 소년도 있었다. 그 아이는 그 배의 심부름꾼이었다. 소년들이 배를 탔을 때, 선원들 대부분은 시내로 술을 마시러 가고 없었다. 선장은 아직 거기에 없었다. 오직 모코와 선원 한 사람만이 거기에서 소년들을 맞이하기 위해 있었다. 일단 소년들이 잠자리에 들자, 그 선원도 모코에게 일을 맡기고 시내로 갔다. 그러나 모코는 너무 피곤해서 깨어 있을 수 없었다.

p.12~13

어찌 된 일이었는지 모르지만, 그 배를 항구 벽에 묶어두었던 밧줄이 풀렸다. 아무도 그 배가 바다로 미끄러져 나가는 것을 눈치채지 못했다. 모코가 맨 먼저 잠에서 깨어났고, 다른 아이들을 깨우기 위해 그가 할 수 있는 한 크게 소리쳤다. 고든, 브리잉, 도니판, 그리고 몇몇 아이들이 일어났다. 그들은 도움을

요청했지만, 너무 멀리 나와서 아무도 그들의 소리를 들을 수 없었다. 바람은 그 배를 곧장 바다로, 즉 태평양으로 떠밀었다. 소년들은 불빛 하나가 자기들을 향해 다가오는 것을 보고는 도와달라고 소리쳤다. 그것은 증기선이었는데, 거대하고 소음이 심했다. 그 배에 탄 누구도 아주 작은 그 배를 알아차리거나 자기네 배의 엔진 소음 너머로 소년들의 외침을 듣지 못했다.

p.14~15

그 증기선은 소년들의 배에 너무 가까이 다가와서 배의 이름이 적힌 표지판 조각을 떨어뜨렸다. 다행히, 그 작은 배는 침몰하는 대신에 똑바로 있었지만, 증기선은 그냥 지나가 버렸고…… 소년들은 거세지는 폭풍우 속으로 항해해 나갔다. 물론, 소년들의 가족은 그들을 찾았지만, 배의 표지판 조각을 발견하고는 그 배가 침몰했다고 짐작했다. 슬픔에 잠긴 그들은 수색을 포기했다.

몇 주 후, 소년들은 그들이 또 다른 폭풍우 속에 있다는 것을 알았다. 배가 엄청난 파도를 뚫고 항해를 계속하는 동안, 하루하

루는 인내의 시험이었다. 날씨가 이렇게 험악할 때
는 배를 꼭 붙잡고 돛들이 찢어져 나가지 않기를 바
라는 것밖에는 할 수 있는 게 없었다.

p.16~17

갑판에는 고든, 브리앙, 도니판, 그리고 모코가 서서
타륜을 꼭 붙잡고 배를 조종하기 위해 모두 애쓰고
있었다. 모코의 피부는 그들 머리 위에 있는 구름들
처럼 검은 반면, 도니판은 두려움으로 창백해 보였
다. 이들 넷은 모두 나이가 열두 살에서 열네 살 사
이였다. 갑판 아래 선실들에는 이들보다 어린 열한
명의 소년과 개 한 마리가 있었다.

갑자기 모코가 외쳤다. "육지다! 육지가 보여!" "정말
이야?" 도니판이 이른 아침의 어둠 속을 뚫어지게
바라보면서 물었다. 그는 자기가 맞길 바라면서 다
른 사람들이 말하는 것은 항상 무엇이든 의심했다.
틀림없이 그는 자신이 다른 누구보다 낫다고 생각하
는 듯이 보였기 때문에 나머지 소년들 중 몇몇은 그
를 '도니판 경'이라고 불렀다. "응, 확실해." 모코가
대답했다. "돛대의 오른쪽을 봐." "육지야!" 브리앙이
소리쳤다. "정말이야!" 그러고 나서, 그들 모두는 수
평선 위에 있는 길쭉하고 나지막한 좁은 육지를 보
았다.

p.18~19

브리앙은 타고난 지도자이자 머리 회전이 빠른 아이
였다. 그는 만약
배가 암초에 부
딪힌다면 모두
가 갑판 위에 있
는 것이 더 안전
할 거라고 판단
했다. 그는 갑판
아래의 선실들

로 이어지는 문을 열고 소리쳤다. "얘들아, 모두 갑
판 위로 올라와." 곧바로 개가 뛰쳐나왔고, 열한 명
의 소년들이 전부 그 뒤를 따랐다. 그들이 그들 주위
의 파도를 보았을 때 가장 어린아이들이 소리를 지
르기 시작했다.

갑자기 엄청난 충격이 있었다. 배는 암초에 좌초했
다. 파도가 배 주위를 소용돌이 치면서 배를 다시 완
전히 들어 올렸지만, 파도는 배를 좀 더 멀리 실어
날라 얕은 바다의 어느 모래사장 위에 떨어뜨렸다.
배는 육지에 닿았으나, 대체 어떤 종류의 육지였을
까? 그것은 그들이 마을이나 시내 같은 어떤 일종의
정착지에 도착할 때까지 육로로 이동할 수 있는 경
우에는 대륙일 수도 있었다. 하지만 만약 그것이 섬
이라면, 안전하게 항해할 수 있는 배 없이는 떠날 방
법이 없기 때문에 상황은 더욱 복잡해질 것이었다.

p.20~21

소년들은 서
둘러 배에서
빠져나왔고,
배를 바다 밖
으로 내놓기
위해 그것을
끌고 물을 헤
치며 해안으
로 걸었다. 배는 박살나고 산산조각 나 그곳에서 멀
리 항해할 방법이 없었다. 해안에는 인적이 없었다.
"우선, 우린 음식과 지낼 곳이 필요해." 브리앙이 말
했다. "그런 후에, 다음에 우리가 뭘 할지 생각해낼
수 있어." 브리앙과 고든은 해변을 걸어 올라가 숲으
로 들어갔고, 그곳에서 절벽을 발견했다. 그들은 개
울에 다다를 때까지 절벽을 따라갔다. 개울 반대편
에는 습지가 있었다. 거기에는 비바람을 피할 장소
가 없는 것이 확실했다. 실망한 소년들은 난파선으
로 돌아왔다. 그들은 당분간 그곳에서 지내야만 할
것이었다. 다행히도, 침구류, 의류, 그리고 조리기구
들이 여전히 배에 있었다. 거기에는 심지어 식량도
있어서, 모코는 그것으로 훌륭한 식사를 만들었다.

모코는 모두를 안전하고 편안하게 만들곤 했던 실용적인 재주를 많이 지닌 대단히 합리적이고 도움이 되는 소년이었다. 브리앙의 남동생 자크를 제외하고 모두가 놀라울 만큼 쾌활해 보였는데, 자크는 매우 우울해 보였다. 이튿날 아침, 소년들은 그들의 식량을 살펴보았다. 브리앙과 고든은 그들이 두 달은 버틸 만큼 충분하다고 판단했지만, 그들이 이곳에서 얼마 동안이나 살아남아야 할지를 몰랐기 때문에 다른 식량 공급원들을 찾을 필요가 있었다.

그들은 바닷새들의 알을 모았고, 배에 있던 낚싯줄을 이용하여 물고기를 잡았다. 그들은 또 바다 근처의 바위에서 조개류들도 찾았다. 배에는 식량뿐만 아니라 밧줄, 돛, 지도, 성냥 같은 다른 물자들도 있었다. 따뜻하고 방수가 되는 옷도 많았다. 그리고 총기들도 있었지만, 브리앙은 그것들을 사용할 일이 절대 없기를 바랐다! 그들은 숲에서 거처를 찾기 위해 노력해야 한다고 결정했다. 해변의 날씨는 너무 험악했고, 겨울이 오면 그들은 그곳에서 지낼 수가 없을 것이었다.

브리앙, 도니판, 서비스, 그리고 윌콕스는 개, 판을 함께 데리고 답사를 하기 위해 길을 나섰다. 판단력이 아주 뛰어난 고든은 나머지 소년들을 돌보기 위해 뒤에 남았다. 서비스는 약간 게을렀지만 대체로 상냥하고 함께 어울리기가 쉬운 마음씨 착한 소년이었다. 네 명의 답사자는 해변을 따라 출발했다. 그들

은 꽤 힘들게 절벽을 올라가 반대편으로 재빨리 기어 내려갔는데, 거기에서 숲을 더 발견했다. 그 소년들은 걷고 또 걸었다. 숲은 끝이 없는 것 같아 보였다.

숲 한복판에서 그들은 우연히 강을 만났고, 그곳에서 놀라운 발견을 했다. "이거 봐." 서비스가 바위 몇 개를 빤히 쳐다보면서 말했다. "누군가가 이 바위들로 다리 같은 걸 만들어 놨어." "그 바위들은 폭풍우에 의해 거기로 휩쓸려 왔을 수도 있어." 브리앙이 말했다. "그게 근처에 사람들이 있다고 증명하진 않아."

하지만 소년들은 그날 밤에 숲에서 야영하기 위해 자리를 잡을 때 매우 주의를 기울였다. 그들은 만약 주변에 사람들이 있을 경우를 대비해 모닥불을 피우지 않기로 결정했다. 그들은 누구의 주의도 끌고 싶지 않았지만, 그건 야외에서 오직 차가운 음식과 함께 몹시 추운 밤을 보낸다는 의미였다. 이튿날 아침, 소년들은 일찍 일어나 숲을 답사하기 위해 약간 안쪽으로 더 들어갔다. 놀랍게도, 그들은 그들이 나뭇잎과 나무로 만든 오두막 가까이에서 잠을 잤다는 것을 발견했다.

"분명히 이건 근처에 사람들이 있다는 뜻이야." 도니판이 속삭였다. "이 오두막은 오랫동안 사용되지 않은 것처럼 낡아 보여." 브리앙이 말했다. "하지만 주변에 사람들이 있을 수도 있어." 서비스가 걱정스럽게 말했다. "그리고 우린 그들이 착한지 나쁜지도 모르잖아." "그들이 식인종이 아니라면 좋겠어." 윌콕스가 속삭였다.

2장. 발견한 것들과 비밀

p.30~31

소년들은 마침내 숲의 끝에 다다랐고, 그 너머에 모래사장과 광활하게 펼쳐진 바다를 발견했다. "이건 섬이야." 브리앙은 실망하여 꽤 짜증이 나서 소리쳤다.

"봐, 여긴 바다고 반대편에는 해변의 흔적이 없어." "난 그렇게 생각하지 않아." 많은 것에 대해 브리앙과 의견이 전혀 다른 도니판이 말했다. "내 생각엔 우리가 좀 더 멀리 탐사해봐야 해." 브리앙은 비록 도니판과 그의 따지기 좋아하는 태도에 점점 화가 나고 있었지만, 그는 동의했다. 소년들은 야생 동물이나 사람들을 대비하여 그들 주변을 조심스럽게 살피면서 다시 출발했다.

p.32~33

마침내 그들은 바다 너머에 모래사장을 발견했다. 그들은 조그만 언덕을 올라갔고, 도니판이 맨 먼저 꼭대기에 도착했다. "이건 절대 바다가 아니야." 그

가 말했다. "이건 거대한 호수인데, 그 얘긴 우리가 섬에 있는 게 아니란 뜻이야, 브리앙." 브리앙은 그것에 대해 여전히 확신할 수 없었지만, 그들이 길을 떠나기 전에 고든이 그에게 도니판과 다투

지 않도록 노력해달라고 부탁했기 때문에 당장은 조용히 있었다. 그들이 숲 근처의 호숫가로 돌아왔을 때, 판이 이상하게 행동하기 시작했다. 그는 짖어대면서 나무들과 소년들 사이를 왔다 갔다 뛰어 다니며 호숫가에 있는 한 무리의 나무들을 향해 달려갔다. 그는 소년들이 그를 따라오기를 바라는 것처럼 보였고, 그래서 그들은 그렇게 했다. 그들은 몇 개의 글자와 연도가 새겨져 있는 나무 한 그루를 발견했다.

FB
1807

p.34~35

소년들은 그것을 유심히 살펴보았고, 그것이 어떤 의미인지를 알아내려고 애쓰는 동안, 판은 다시 급히 가버리더니 사라졌다. 그들은 판이 다시 짖는 소리를 듣고 그를 쫓아 절벽의 맨 아랫부분에 있는 관목 쪽으로 갔다. 관목들 뒤쪽에는 가로질러 자란 나뭇가지들에 의해 감춰진 동굴의 입구가 있었다. "조심해." 도니판이 말했다. "그 안에 뭔가가, 아니면 누군가가 살고 있을 수도 있어!" "우리는 그 공기가 호흡하기에 괜찮은지도 확인해야 해." 브리앙이 경고했다.

소년들은 주의하며 걷고 조심스레 숨을 쉬면서 동굴 안으로 들어갔다. 바닥은 말라 있었고 모래가 덮여 있었으며, 공기는 숨을 쉬기에 좋았다. 놀랍게도, 그 안에는 철제 컵과 주전자가 놓인 탁자가 하나 있었다. 심지어 거기에는 비록 오래전에 시간을 알리는 것을 멈추긴 했지만, 시계도 하나 벽에 있었다.

p.36~37

소년들이 보기에 언젠가 어떤 사람이 여기 살았었다는 것은 분명했는데, 얼마나 오래전인지는 알기가 어려웠다. 밖에서는 판이 여전히 짖고 있었다. 소년

들이 그를 보기 위해 밖으로 나왔더니, 섬뜩하게도 강둑에 해골이 하나 놓여 있었다! 소년들은 그 광경에 깜짝 놀랐다. 이 사람은 틀림없이 조난 당했었고, 그 동굴 안에서 살았던 것이 틀림없지만, 그의 해골이 아직 여기 있다는 사실은 그가 결코 이곳을 떠나지 못했다는 것을 의미했다.

그건 그들도 결코 섬을 떠날 수 없을지도 모른다는 뜻이기 때문에, 그런 생각을 하자 브리앙은 오싹한 기분이 들었다. 그럼에도 불구하고, 만약 이 남자가 그 동굴 안에서 살 수 있었다면, 그들도 더 좋은 계획을 생각해낼 때까지 그 동굴 안에서 살 수 있을 것이다. 동굴은 건조했고, 모든 소년들이 생활할 수 있을 만큼 컸다.

그들이 또 한 번의 수색을 하기 위해 내부로 돌아갔을 때 많은 글자가 있는 책을 발견했다. 이름인 프랑수아 보두앙을 제외하고는 그 글자들을 읽기 불가능 했다. FB, 바로 나무에 새겨진 것과 똑같은 머리글자였다! "그 해골은 프랑수아 보두앙이 틀림없어." 브리앙이 말했다. 도니판이 갑자기 외쳤다. "지도를 발견했어! 여기 책의 페이지 사이에 감춰져 있었어!"

"프랑수아가 그걸 그린 게 틀림없어." 브리앙은 더 가까이 살펴보기 위해 도니판의 어깨너머로 몸을 기울이면서 말했다. 그것은 그곳이 실제로 섬이란 것을 증명하는 전체 지역의 지도였다. "그러니까 네가 옳았어, 브리앙." 도니판이 우울하게 말했다. "이곳은 섬이야, 그러니까 우린 배 없인 여길 떠날 수 없어."

소년들은 프랑수아를 위해 무덤을 팠고, 그곳에서 그의 영혼을 위해 기도했다. 그러고는, 고든에게 그 동굴에 대해서 말해 주려고 서둘러 돌아갔다. 그들은 돌아오는 길에 그 지도를 이용해 돌아가는 길을 찾으려고 애썼음에도 길을 잃었다. 밤이 되자, 그들은 자기들의 위치를 알 방법도 없이 숲 속에서 또 하룻밤을 마주했다. 그때, 밤의 고요함 속에서 갑작스러운 탕 하는 소리가 나고 빛이 번쩍했다. 고든이 돌아오는 길을 알려주기 위해 배에서 신호탄을 쏘아 올린 것이었다! 소년들은 다행스럽게도 신호탄 방향으로 서둘러 갔고 한 시간 안에 배로 돌아왔다.

모두 그 동굴로 가서 생활하는 것이 좋은 생각이라고 여겼고, 거기에 프랑스 사람이 살았기 때문에 그들은 그곳을 프랑스 동굴이라고 불렀다. 그들은 모든 것을 동굴로 운반하기 위해 뗏목을 만들었고, 그것을 타고 강을 따라 해변에서 동굴로 갔다. 여전히 말이 없고 우울해 보이는 브리앙의 동생 자크를 제외하고는 그곳에 도착하자 모두 아주 좋아했다. 자크는 항상 유쾌하고 지신만만한 아이로 알려져 있었기 때문에 그것은 그에게는 특이한 일이었다.

"너 뭔가를 감추고 있구나." 브리앙이 자크에게 속삭였다. "아니면, 어디 아프니?" 자크는 그냥 고개를 가로저었지만 그것에 대해서는 어떤 것도 말하기를 거부했다. 소년들은 배에서 모든 침구와 탁자를 동굴 안으로 가져왔고, 따라서 그들은 동굴 안에서 기분 좋고 아늑했다. 모코는 훌륭한 식사를 만들었으며, 그날 밤 동굴 안에는 파티 분위기가 났다.

시간이 지나면서, 소년들은 프랑스 동굴에서의 생활

에 적응했다. 도니판은 언제나 말다툼을 일으켰지만, 고든이 가까스로 모든 것을 진정시켰다. 그는 배에서 가져온 책들로 수업을 했고, 모두 앉아서 들었다. 소년들은 배에서 가져온 연장들로 동굴을 더 크게 만들었다. 다행히 바위는 그들이 조금씩 쪼아낼 수 있을 정도로 부드러워서 그들은 곧 바위를 파냈다. 그리고 그들은 밖을 내다보고 신선한 공기가 동굴 안으로 흘러들어올 수 있도록 하려고 좁다란 창문을 두 개 만들었다. 밖의 홍수와 폭풍우에도 불구하고, 소년들은 모두 안전했다.

p.44~45
이제 소년들은 생활할 더 큰 동굴이 생기자 섬의 주요 부분들에 이름을 붙이기로 했다. "우리 이 섬을 체어맨 섬이라고 부르자." 고든이 제안했다. "우리 학교를 운영하시는 이사장님 이름을 따서 말이야. 그분이 우리를 위해 이 항해를 준비하셨으니까 그분 이름을 따서 섬의 이름을 짓는 거지." 그들은 배가 난파되었던 해변을 스쿠너 만이라고, 이름 지었는데, 스쿠너는 그들이 타고 항해했던 배의 종류였기 때문이다. "우리는 지도자가 필요해." 브리앙이 말했다. "그리고 내 생각에 그건 네가 해야 해, 고든." 대

부분의 아이가 브리앙의 말에 동의해서 고든이 체어맨 섬의 지도자가 되었다.
겨울이 오자, 날씨는 몹시 추워졌다. 눈이 너무 많이 쌓여서 아무도 동굴을 떠날 수 없었다. 고든은 모두를 빨래하는 것과 책들에서 배우는 것으로 계속 바쁘게 만들었다. 눈이 녹자, 소년들은 밖으로 나가 식량을 사냥했다. 섬의 여기저기에는 동물들이 많았고, 도니판은 특히 총으로 그것들을 쏘는 것을 잘했다.

p.46~47

브리앙은 그들이 섬을 떠날 수 있도록 배를 만드는 일에 대해 말했지만, 고든은 그곳에서 사는 것을 좋아했고 모두를 계속 편안하게 해 주기 위해 더 많은 계획을 세웠다. 고든은 훌륭한 지도자였지만, 도니판은 그와 브리앙을 질투했기 때문에 그들 두 사람에 대해 불평하기 시작했다. 어느 날, 그는 심지어 게임을 하다가 브리앙과 싸우기 시작했다. 고든이 와서 그 두 사람을 떼어놓아야 했다. "고든, 왜 네가 지도자여야 하는 건데?" 도니판이 화난 목소리로 말했다. "난 너보다 더 나은 지도자가 될 수 있고, 내가 지도자가 되어야 한다고 생각해."
그의 친구들인 윌콕스와 웹, 그리고 그의 사촌인 크로스가 도니판의 말에 동의했다. 그들은 도니판이 새로운 지도자가 되어야 한다고 다른 소년들을 설득하기 위해 애쓰며 돌아다녔다. 크로스는 언제나 도니판을 존경했고, 그의 사촌이 말하는 것은 모두 했다. 웹과 윌콕스는 겨우 열두 살이었고, 특별히 똑똑하지는 않았다. 그들은 서로 다투고 다른 사람들이 그들을 위해 일을 하게 만드는 것을 좋아했다. 이들은 도니판이 그의 주변에 모으는 종류의 소년들, 즉 그가 말하는 것을 의문 없이 행할 소년들이었다. 나머지 소년들 일부는 그들의 말을 들었고, 또 일부는 도니판과 그의 친구들을 무시했다.

p.48~49
브리앙은 여전히 그의 동생 자크가 걱정스러웠는데, 그 아이는 점점 더 우울해지고 있었다. 마침내, 자크는 브리앙에게 자신의 비밀을 말했다. "형은 나를 용서할지도 몰라." 그가 말했

다. "그렇지만 다른 아이들은 그럴 거라고 생각 안해." "그런데 너 무슨 짓을 한 거니?" 브리앙이 물었다. "이제 곧 알게 될 거야." 이렇게 말하면서 자크는 울기 시작했다.

이제 소년들은 몇몇 동물과 새들을 잡았다. 그들은 그것들을 위해 농장 울타리를 만들었다. 모코는 새 알과 라마같은 동물인 비쿠냐의 젖으로 몇몇 훌륭한 음식들을 요리했다. 심지어 그는 단풍나무 수액으로 설탕 시럽을 만들어내기도 해서 모두 잘 먹었다! "나는 섬 동쪽에 가서 살펴 볼거야." 브리앙이 말했다. "그러면, 그쪽에 어떤 배가 지나가는지 볼 수 있으니까." 그는 모코와 자크를 데리고 갔다. 그들은 더 큰 난파선에서 가져온 작은 배를 타고 떠났다.

p.50~51

강을 따라 오랫동안 여행한 후에 그들은 동쪽 해안에 도착했다. 그곳에는 몇 개의 바위만 있는 모래사장이 있었지만, 하루종일 머물면서 지켜보아도 그쪽으로는 배가 한 척도 지나가지 않았다. 브리앙은 마치 그 장소가 그를 속인 것처럼 느꼈기 때문에 그곳을 사기 만이라고 불렀다. 그는 망원경을 통해 살펴보다가 수평선 위에 있는 이상한 것을 보면서 얼굴을 찡그렸다. 그것은 구름처럼 보였으나 하늘은 맑았다. 비록 모코도 그것이 보인다고 말했지만, 브리앙은 그게 무엇인지 알 수 없었다. 얼마 후, 브리앙과 자크는 그들이 보트를 타고 동굴로 돌아갈 수 있게

조류가 바뀌기를 기다리도록 모코를 남겨둔 채, 그들 끼리 만 산책하러 나갔다.

모코는 브리앙과 자크가 자크의 비밀에 대해 말하는 것을 엿듣지 않을 수 없었다. "네가 그랬구나!" 브리앙은 숨이 턱 막혔고, 목소리는 움찔했다. "미안해." 자크가 말하고 다시 울기 시작했다. "다른 애들한테는 절대로 말해서는 안 돼." 브리앙이 말했다.

p.54~55

브리앙, 자크, 그리고 모코가 동굴로 돌아왔을 때, 생활은 보통 때처럼 계속됐다. 도니판은 계속 모든 아이와 다투었고, 모든 일에 대해 불평했다. 이제 고든이 섬의 지도자가 된 지 꼬박 1년이 되었다. "새로운 지도자를 뽑을 때가 됐어." 자기가 새 지도자로 선출되기를 바라는 도니판이 말했다. 하지만 대신에 브리앙이 선출되었고, 또 한 번의 겨울 동안 도니판은 점점 더 화가 났다.

다시 여름이 왔을 때, 도니판은 더는 그것을 참을 수 없었다. "난 네가 말하는 대로 하는 게 싫증이 나." 그는 브리앙에게 쏘아붙이고 크로스, 윌콕스, 그리고 웹을 데리고 사기 만으로 떠났다. "우린 다른 애들은 필요 없어." 그가 말했다. "우린 우리 힘으로 여기서 완벽하게 잘 살 수 있어."

p.56~57

사기 만에서의 첫째 날 밤은 요란한 천둥소리와 번쩍이는 번개를 동반한 심한 폭풍우가 쳤다. 도니판과 친구들이 해변 가장자리에 있는 숲에서 머무르고 있을 때, 윌콕스는 뭔가 이상한 것을 발견했다. "저

게 뭐지?" 그는 해변 위에 있는 크고 어두운 형체를 가리키며 소리쳤다. 그것은 배처럼 보였다. 소년들은 살펴보러 재빨리 달려갔고, 그게 배라는 것을 알았다.

모래 위에 몸체 두 개가 배 바로 옆에 누워 있었다. 소년들은 그곳에 머물며 돕기 위해 애써야 한다고 생각했지만, 폭풍우가 아주 사나워서 너무 무서웠다. 그들은 황급히 나무들이 있는 피난처로 돌아왔다. 밤새, 그들은 멀리서 나는 비명 소리를 들은 것 같았지만, 번개가 멈추자 너무 어두워 아무것도 볼 수 없었다.

p.58~59

아침이 되어 날이 밝자, 소년들은 배를 살펴보러 갔다. 하지만 두 몸체는 사라졌고, 그들이 야생 동물들에 의해 끌려간 흔적도 없었다. "조류가 그들을 휩쓸어간 게 분명해." 도니판이 말했다.

배는 한쪽 측면이 완전히 파손되어 있었지만, 뒤쪽에서 그들은 아직 '세번'이라는 이름을 읽을 수 있었다. 또한, 거기에는 '샌프란시스코'라는 글자도 쓰여 있었는데, 그 배가 출항했던 항구를 가리키는 것이었다. "이건 미국에서 온 거야." 도니판이 말했다. "난 그 얘기가 우리가 미국 해안 가까이에 있다는 뜻인지 궁금하네."

p.60~61

다시 프랑스 동굴로 돌아가 보면, 모두가 슬펐다. 그들은 도니판과 그의 친구들이 아주 떠나버리지 않기를 바랐다. 하지만 생각할 다른 일들이 있었는데, 어떤 배가 그 섬을 지나갈 경우를 대비한 신호의 필요성 같은 것이었다. "연을 하나 만들자." 브리앙이 제안했다. "그게 하늘 높이 올라갈 거고, 만약 어떤 배들이 지나간다면 그걸 보게 될 거야." 더 어린 소년들은 브리앙의 생각에 대해 아주 흥미로워했으며 거대한 연을 만들며 즐거운 시간을 보냈다.

그들은 그것을 배에서 가져온 무거운 금속 원치에 붙들어 맸다. 그들은 연이 날아가지 못하도록 원치를 땅에 고정했다. 소년들이 막 연을 띄울 준비가 되었을 때, 판은 다시 짖으면서 숲을 향해 달려갔다. "그가 이번엔 뭘 발견한 거지?" 모든 소년이 그 개를 쫓아가면서, 고든이 물었다. 이번에는 판이 그들을 나무 밑에 누워 있는 한 여인에게로 이끌었는데, 그녀는 의식이 없었지만 살아 있었다. 그들은 그녀를 동굴로 데려와 브랜디로 입술을 적셔주었다.

p.62~63

40대로 보였던 그 여인이 깨어났을 때, 그녀는 그들에게 자신의 이야기를 했다. "내 이름은 케이트란다." 그녀가 말했다. "내 주인과 그 부인께서 칠레로 항해하는 '세번'이라고 불리는 배에 나를 데리고 승선했을 때 나는 미국에서 하녀였단다." 케이트는 소년들에게 '세번'호의 선원들에 대해 모두 말해 주었다. 그들은 배와 배 위의 모든 것들의 주도권을 차지할 수 있도록 선장인 그녀의 주인과 그의 부인을 살해했다.

그들의 우두머리는 월스턴이라고 불렸고, 다른 선원도 대부분 거의 나쁜 사람들이었다. 비록 그들 가운데 한 명인 포브스란 사람은 나머지 다른 자들보다는 덜 잔인했지만 그들은 월스턴이 하라는 대로 했다. 포브스는 그들을 설득하여 케이트의 목숨을 구해 주었다. 또한, 그 사내들은 선주인 에반스의 목숨도 살려주었는데, 그는 선장 다음으로 배의 지휘권을 가진 사람이었다. 그들은 항해하려면 그가 필요했다.

p.64~65
케이트는 소년들에게 어떻게 배에 불이 붙었는지와 그 불길을 피하기 위해 배 밖으로 뛰어내렸다가 죽은 한 사내에 대해 말해 주었다. 불이 어떻게 시작되었는지는 아무도 몰랐지만, 불길이 너무 사나워 배는 완전히 타서 침몰했다. 다행히, 그들이 뛰어내려 탈 수 있는 구명정이 하나 있었다. 이것이 그 선원들과 케이트를 태우고 체어맨 섬의 해변으로 휩쓸려왔

던 배였다. 그 구명정이 해변에 닿자 케이트는 해변으로 내동댕이쳐졌고, 얼마 후에 겨우 깨어나 눈에 띄지 않고 달아났다. 그 사내들은 아마도 그녀가 지금 죽었다고 생각할 거였다.

브리앙은 그 섬에 위험한 사내들이 있다는 말을 듣고 공포에 휩싸였다! "우린 도니판과 나머지 애들을 찾아야 해." 그가 소리쳤다. "우린 그 애들이 더 안전할 수 있는 동굴로 다시 데려올 거야." 그와 모코는 그들을 찾으러 길을 나섰는데, 배를 타고 강을 따라 깊고 어두운 숲으로 들어갔다.

p.66~67
도니판과 그의 친구들은 숲에서 꺼져 가는 불 옆에서 야영하고 있었다. 브리앙과 모코가 도착한 그 순간 재규어 한 마리가 도니판에게 달려들었다. 윌콕스가 재규어를 쏘기 위해 총을 잡았지만, 브리앙이 소리쳤다. "쏘지 마!" 그는 칼을 휘둘러 재규어를 베었고, 그 과정에서 브리앙은 어깨에 상처를 입

었다. 재규어가 절뚝거리며 멀어져 가면서, 소년들에게 달아날 기회를 주었다. "서둘러!" 브리앙이 숨을 헐떡이며 자신의 어깨를 움켜잡았다. "가자!" "내 목숨을 구해줘서 고마워." 도니판이 말했다.

p.68~69
브리앙은 그들을 배로 다시 데려가면서 그들에게 위험한 사내들에 대해 말해 주었다. "그게 내가 너한테 총을 쏘지 말라고 했던 이유야, 윌콕스." 그가 설명했다. "그들이 총소리를 들을지도 모르고 이 섬에 자기들만 있는 게 아니란 걸 알게 될지도 모르니까." 다시 한 번 친구가 된 브리앙과 도니판은 배를 타고 동굴로 돌아왔고, 15명의 소년이 모두 다시 모였다. 모두들 발견되지 않도록 아주 조심해야 했다. 브리앙은 위험한 사내들이 그들을 발견할 경우에 대비하여 그들이 동굴에서 멀리 떨어지는 것을 허락하지 않았다.

그때, 브리앙에게 굉장히 좋은 생각이 하나 있었다. "우리는 이 연을 공중에 높이 보낼 수 있어." 그가 말했다. "한 아이가 그것과 함께 올라갈 수 있어. 그 애가 섬 전체를 볼 수 있을 거고, 그 사내들이 정확히 어디 있는지 볼 수 있을 거야." 나머지 소년들은 그 일이 가능할지도 모른다는 것에 동의했다. 그들은 어떻게 한 소년의 무게를 지탱하면서도 연이 여전히 날게 할 수 있는지를 계산하면서 며칠을 보냈다. 그들은 한 소년이 그 안에 설 수 있도록 연 밑에 매달 바구니를 하나 만들었다.

p.70~71
"누가 그걸 타고 올라가지?" 고든이 물었다. 자크가 자원했지만, 도니판과 다른 소년들 중 몇몇도 자원했다. "꼭 내가 해야 해." 자크가 고집했다. "왜냐하면, 내가 저질렀던 잘못을 만회하고 싶으니까." 마침내, 그는 오클랜드 항구에서 밧줄을 풀어버린 사람이 그였다고 고백했다. 배가 먼 곳으로 흘러왔던 일

은 그의 잘못이었다. "장난을 치려고 했던 거였어." 그가 작고 미안한 목소리로 말했다.

"걱정 마." 도니판이 말했다. "그건 실수였고, 우린 널 용서할 거야." 이제는 자크가 왜 그렇게 지금껏 매우 슬퍼했는지 모두 알게 되었다. 그들 모두는 그가 바구니에 타고 올라가 섬을 살펴보는 일에 동의했다. 하지만 브리앙은 자기 동생이 그토록 위험한 일을 하는 것을 원치 않았다. 그래서, 자크가 바구니에 막 발을 들여놓으려는 때에 브리앙이 먼저 올라타 연을 띄워 올리라고 명령했다!

p.74~75

브리앙과 연은 밤하늘로 높이높이 올라갔고, 곧 어둠 속으로 사라졌다. 연은 스스로 멀리 날아갈 수 없게 밧줄에 묶여 있었다. 브리앙은 그 밧줄이 팽팽히 당겨지고 산들바람을 맞으며 섬 상공을 맴돌 때까지 10분 동안 올라갔다. 그는 아래에 있는 모든 것이 아주 잘 보였다. 그가 맨 처음 본 것은 동쪽에 있는 불빛이었지만, 그것은 너무 멀리 떨어져 있어서 섬에 있는 것일 수가 없었다.

"저건 화산인가?" 그는 궁금했다. "어쩌면 저쪽에 육지가 있을 거야!" 그는 사기 만에서 보았던 하얀 지점을 기억하고는 어쩌면 거기에 빙하로 덮인 섬이 있을지도 모른다고 생각했다.

p.76~77

그때, 그는 또 다른 불을 발견했는데, 이번에는 훨씬 더 가까웠다. 그것은 브리앙에게 그 사내들이 아직도 체어맨 섬에 있다는 것을 보여 주었다. 그는 나머지 아이들에게 자기와 연을 다시 땅으로 끌어 내리라고 알리기 위해 밧줄을 당겼다. 그런데, 연이 아래로 내려지고 있을 때, 갑작스러운 돌풍이 불었다. 그것은 밧줄을 끊고 브리앙을 바구니에서 내쳐버릴 정도로 강했다! 그가 공중에서 떨어지자, 모두 소리치며 그의 이름을 불렀지만, 다행히도 그는 호수에 떨어져 다치지 않고 호숫가로 헤엄쳐 나왔다. 연은 그것을 아래로 내려오도록 해 주는 브리앙의 무게가 없어지자, 거대한 새처럼 하늘로 날아가 버렸다.

폭풍우 치던 어느 날 밤, 동굴 안에 있던 소년들과 케이트는 밖에서 도움을 청하는 목소리를 들었다. "에반스 목소리 같아." 케이트가 말했

다. "그는 좋은 사람이라 그가 우리를 봐도 안전해." 그래서 소년들은 에반스가 동굴로 들어오는 것을 허락했다. 그는 케이트가 결국 살아 있는 것을 발견하고 몹시 좋아했다. "'세번'호의 구명정은 수리될 수 있어." 그가 말했다. "하지만, 그자들은 그걸 할 수 있는 연장이 없어서 아직도 여기에 있는 거야." "근데, 우린 연장이 있어요." 도니판이 말했다. "우리가 그걸 수리할 수 있어요!"

p.78~79

에반스는 그들에게 그 위험한 사내들이 섬에 떨어진 연을 발견했다고 말해 주었다. 그러고 나서, 그들은 다른 누군가가 이 섬에 있다는 것을 알았고, 곧이어 이 동굴을 발견했었다. 그들은 동굴을 빼앗고, 그 안에 있는 모든 것들을 훔쳐가기 위해 공격을 계획하고 있는 중이었다. 에반스는 그들에게 가까운 곳에 육지가 있다는 얘기도 했는데, 그렇다면 브리앙의 말이 맞았다! "이 섬은 남아메리카 대륙 해안 인근에 있어." 그가 말했다. "그리고 실제 이름은 하노버 섬이야." 그래서 소년들은 그 사내들이 그들을 제지하

는 일 없이 그들을 구명정에 도달하게 한다면, 그들의 연장으로 구명정을 수리할 계획을 세우기 시작했다. 그러면, 그들은 항해에 나설 것이고, 어쩌면 집으로 돌아가는 길을 찾을 수 있을 것이다. 하지만 먼저, 그들은 그 사내들을 처리해야 했는데, 그것이 쉬운 일은 아닐 것이었다.

어느 날 저녁, 두 사내가 동굴로 왔을 때 악당들의 공격이 이상할 만큼 조용한 방법으로 시작되었다. 그들은 난파선의 선원들인 척하며 그들의 이름이 포브스와 록이라고 했다. "우릴 도와주겠니?" 포브스가 소리쳤다. "우리에게 음식과 거처를 좀 마련해주면서 말이야." 소년들은 그 사내들의 이야기를 믿는 척하며 그들을 동굴로 들어오게 했다. 그들은 그 사내들을 붙잡고 싶었다.

일단, 그 사내들이 동굴 안으로 들어오자, 소년들은 그들을 창고로 밀어넣고 거기에 포로로 잡아두었다. 그 사내들은 달아나려 했으나, 에반스가 포브스를 붙잡았다. 불행히도, 록은 탈출해 도망쳐서 다른 사내들에게로 돌아갔다.

이튿날, 다른 사내들의 도착을 알리는 총소리가 났다. 나이가 더 있는 소년들은 동굴 밖으로 뛰쳐나갔고, 엄청난 전투가 벌어졌다. 많은 총싸움과 칼싸움이 있었고, 가여운 도니판은 칼에 찔리고 말았다. 그는 마치 죽을 것처럼 보였다. "그를 동굴로 데려가." 고든이 소리쳤지만, 사내들 가운데 몇몇은 벌써 동굴로 들어간 뒤였다. 그 위험한 사내들의 우두머리인 월스턴이 자크를 움켜잡았다. 그는 자크를 동굴 근처의 강에 정박시켜두었던 소년들의 배에 태워 데려가려고 했다.

포브스가 재빨리 동굴 밖으로 뛰쳐나가 월스턴을 공격했지만 싸우다가 죽임을 당했다. 모든 것

이 소년들에게 불리한 것처럼 보였을 때, 예상치 못했던 일이 벌어졌다. 모코가 동굴 안 창고에 숨어 있었고, 그 사내들에게 발각되지 않고 남아 있었다. 이제, 그는 총을 가지고 창고에서 나왔다. 그는 동굴의 창문들을 통해 총을 여러 발 쏘았다.

사내들 몇몇은 죽임을 당했고, 다른 사내들은 상처를 입었다. 그들은 숲 속으로 탈출했으나, 거기에서 부상 때문에 죽었다. 소년들은 판이 그들을 시체들 있는 곳으로 데려갔기 때문에 이 사실을 알았다. 소년들은 전투에서 이겼지만, 도니판은 심각하게 아팠다. 케이트는 나뭇잎들로 그의 상처를 치료했고, 통증과 열이 있는 며칠간 그를 밤낮으로 보살폈다.

p.86〜87

한편, 소년들은 연장, 무기, 그리고 식량을 사기 만으로 옮겼다. 그들은 '세 번'호의 구명정을 수리할 준비가 되었다. 그들은 수리를 위해 열심히 일했고, 마침내 배가 준비되었다.

케이트의 세심한 간호 덕분에 도니판은 건강이 점점 나아졌으며, 얼마 후에는 다른 아이들과 합류하기 위해 사기 만으로 찾아올 만큼 몸이 좋아졌다. 그 섬에서 거의 2년을 보낸 후에야, 집으로 돌아갈 시도를 할 때가 되었다! 떠나기 전, 소년들은 프랑수아 보두앙의 무덤 곁에 포브스의 무덤을 팠다. 그들은 그 무덤들 옆에서 기도를 드렸고, 잠시 동안 이 용감한 사람들에 대해 생각했다.

p.88〜89

2월 5일, 소년들은 케이트와 에반스를 함께 데리고 구명정에 올랐다. 그들이 출발할 때는 심지어 판도 자랑스럽게 뱃머리에 서 있었다. 바다에서 며칠을 보낸 후, 증기선 한 척이 그들을 발견하고 그들이 맨 처음 항해를 시작했던 뉴질랜드를 향해 데려갔다. 1862년 2월 25일, 그들은 마침내 오클랜드로 돌아왔다. 그들이 살아 있는 모습을 볼 희망을 잃었던 소년들의 가족들은 그들을 보고는 매우 기뻐했다. "우리가 떠난 지 2년이 넘었네." 브리앙이 웃었다. "우린 멋진 방학을 보냈어!"

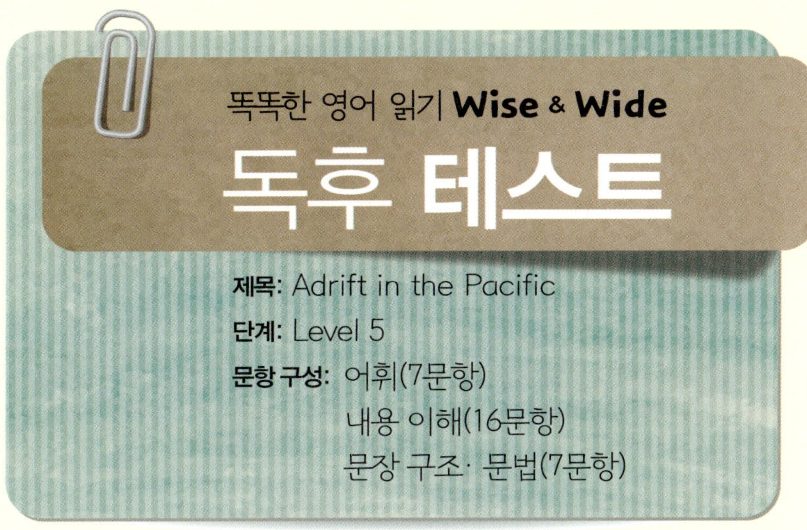

✤ 독후 테스트는 홈페이지(www.darakwon.co.kr)에서 온라인으로도 풀어보실 수 있습니다.
이 경우 점수와 응시 결과에 대한 평가까지 확인하실 수 있습니다.
추가로 제공되는 단어 퀴즈도 풀어보세요.

Adrift in the Pacific 독후 테스트

1. What does "provisions" mean?

   ① weapons
   ② fishing equipment
   ③ food and drink
   ④ medicines

2. What does "cannibal" mean?

   ① a person who lives on islands
   ② a person who is very fierce
   ③ a person who eats other people
   ④ a person who is a ghost

3. What does "reunited" mean in the following sentence?

   > Briant and Doniphan sailed the boat back to the cave and all fifteen boys were <u>reunited</u>.

   ① friendly
   ② enemies
   ③ together again
   ④ happy

4. Which of the following is the wrong past tense form of the verb?

   ① shake – shook
   ② fall – fell
   ③ hide – hid
   ④ begin – begun

5.

> "내 생명을 구해줘서 고마워." 도니판이 말했다.
> → "Thank you for ___________ my life," said Doniphan.

① saving   ② having
③ floating   ④ flying

6.

> 소년들이 배를 탔을 때, 선원들 대부분은 시내로 술을 마시러 가고 없었다.
> → When the boys went ___________ the boat, most of the crew had gone into town for a drink.

① disappeared   ② aboard
③ elected   ④ comfortable

7. What is the common word for the two blanks?

> • It was battered and broken ______, so there was no way of sailing away from here.
> • I must do it because I want to make ______ for the wrong thing I did.

① on   ② up
③ about   ④ of

8. In which season did the voyage begin?

① spring   ② summer
③ fall   ④ winter

9. Why did the boys' families give up searching for them?
  ① They assumed that the boat had sunk.
  ② They didn't care about the boys.
  ③ The weather was too stormy for them to search.
  ④ They knew that the boys would find their own way home.

10. Why did Briant call the younger boys up onto the deck?
  ① He wanted to see if they could see land.
  ② He wanted them to help to hold the wheel.
  ③ He wanted them to be safer if the boat crashed.
  ④ He wanted them to help with the sails.

11. Why did the boys need to look for food?
  ① There was no food on the boat.
  ② The food on the boat had gone bad.
  ③ Some of the boys did not like the food on the boat.
  ④ There was only enough food to last for two months.

12. Which of these things did Phann NOT discover?
  ① a tree with a year and letters scratched on it
  ② an old boat on the shore of the lake
  ③ a cave entrance hidden behind some branches
  ④ a skeleton lying on the bank of the river

13. **Where did François Baudoin come from?**
① New Zealand
② South America
③ France
④ United Kingdom

14. **How did Gordon help the boys who explore the island to find their way back to the boat?**
① He fired a gun.
② He shouted to them.
③ He lit a fire.
④ He sent up a flare.

15. **Who was NOT excited to arrive at the cave?**
① Briant
② Jack
③ Doniphan
④ Gordon

16. **Why was Briant angry with Doniphan?**
① He didn't like it when other people were right and he was wrong.
② He thought that Doniphan had put their lives in danger.
③ He was tired of Doniphan arguing all the time.
④ He blamed Doniphan for leading them the wrong way.

17. Why did Doniphan take Cross, Wilcox, and Webb to Deception Bay?
    ① He was tired of being told what to do by Jack.
    ② He thought he could live there without the others.
    ③ He wanted to try and get away from the island.
    ④ He wanted to live somewhere with more sunlight than the cave.

18. How did the boys stop the kite from floating away?
    ① They tied it to the winch.
    ② They tied it to a tree.
    ③ They tied it to a rock.
    ④ They tied it to the raft.

19. Why did Jack volunteer to go up in the basket with the kite?
    ① He wanted to make up for the wrong thing that he had done.
    ② He wanted to take a closer look at some birds.
    ③ He wanted to show that he was the bravest boy of them all.
    ④ He wanted to get away from all the other boys.

20. Why had the men from the "Severn" NOT left the island?
    ① They didn't know how to mend the lifeboat.
    ② The lifeboat had been washed away.
    ③ They liked the island so much that they wanted to stay.
    ④ They didn't have tools to mend the lifeboat.

21. Why did the boys allow Forbes and Rock into the cave?

① The boys wanted to capture the men.

② The boys didn't know that they were bad men.

③ The boys hoped that the men would help them to mend the boat.

④ The boys could not stop the men from entering the cave.

22. Where did the boys take their tools, weapons, and provisions?

① Schooner Bay

② Deception Bay

③ French Cave

④ into the forest

23. How many people boarded the lifeboat to try to leave the island?

① fourteen

② fifteen

③ sixteen

④ seventeen

※ Choose the wrong part of each sentence. (24~27)

24.
거기에는 비바람을 피할 장소가 없는 것이 확실했다.
→ It was <u>clear</u> <u>that</u> there was no place <u>sheltering</u> there.
  ①   ②   ③   ④

25.
“우리는 공기가 호흡하기에 괜찮은지도 확인해야 한다.” 브리앙이 경고했다.

→ “We must checking that the air is good to breathe, too,” warned Briant.
　　①　　　　②　　　　　　　　③　　　④

26.
그러나 그것은 너무 맹렬해서 배 전체가 불타고 가라앉았다.

→ But it was so fierce it the entire ship burned up and sank.
　　　　　①　②　③　　　　　　　　　　　　　④

27.
포브스가 재빨리 동굴 밖으로 뛰쳐나가 월스턴에게 덤벼들었지만 싸우다가 죽임을 당했다.

→ Forbes rushed out of the cave and attacked Walston, but
　　　　　①　　　　　　　　　　　②

killed in the struggle.
　③　　　　　④

※ Choose the correct sentence that is translated into English. (28~30)

28.
그리고 우린 그들이 좋은 사람들인지 나쁜 사람들인지도 모른다.

① And we don't know if they are good or bad.
② And we don't know if they will be good or bad.
③ And we don't know if they good or bad.
④ And we don't know if they could be good or bad.

29.

① There was even a clock on the wall, though it stopped tell the time long ago.
② There was even a clock on the wall, though it stopped to tell the time long ago.
③ There was even a clock on the wall, though it stopped old the time long ago.
④ There was even a clock on the wall, though it had stopped telling the time long ago.

30.

① The cave was dry, and big enough for all the boys to live in.
② The cave was dry, and enough big for all the boys to live in.
③ The cave was dry, and big for enough all the boys to live in.
④ The cave was dry, and enough to big for all the boys to live in.

✛ 정답과 해설은 홈페이지(www.darakwon.co.kr)를 통해 확인하세요.

Memo

Memo 

Sarah J. Dodd 선생님은…
현재 영국에 거주하시는 베테랑 초등 교사이자 작가이십니다. 호주에서도 수년간 교직 생활을 하셨습니다. 과학 분야 박사 학위와 문예 창작 자격증을 가지고 계십니다. 대표 작품으로는 An Angel Anyway와 Little Angels 시리즈, The Lion Picture Bible, Legs: the tale of a meerkat lost and found 등이 있습니다. 선생님의 동시가 시 선집 Let in the Stars에 수록되어 출간되기도 했습니다. 이외에도 유아들을 위한 그림책과 청소년들을 위한 소설을 집필하고 계십니다.

15소년 표류기
Adrift in the Pacific

원작 Jules Verne
각색 Sarah J. Dodd
펴낸이 정규도

초판 1쇄 인쇄 2017년 1월 16일
초판 1쇄 발행 2017년 1월 23일

편집장 최주연
책임편집 박지영, 장경희
표지·본문 디자인 이은희
전산편집 이은희
일러스트 김혜영
번역 안창열

다락원 경기도 파주시 문발로 211
내용문의 (02)736-2031 내선 510
구입문의 (02)736-2031 내선 250~252
Fax (02)732-2037
출판등록 1977년 9월 16일 제300-1977-23호
Copyright © 2017, 다락원

ISBN 978-89-277-0426-3 18740 / 978-89-277-0371-6 18740(set)

http://www.darakwon.co.kr
다락원 홈페이지를 방문하시면 상세한 출판 정보와 함께 MP3 자료 등 다양한 어학 정보를 얻으실 수 있습니다.